This Side
Of
Tomorrow

Janet Clash Woolridge

TO SOW THE FALLOW SOIL

Winston-Derek Publishers, Inc.
Pennywell Drive—P.O. Box 90883
Nashville, TN 37209

First printing

PUBLISHED BY WINSTON-DEREK PUBLISHERS, INC.
Nashville, Tennessee 37205

Library of Congress Catalog Card No: 87-51042
ISBN: 1-55523-122-5

Printed in the United States of America

Dedication

Dedicated to the memory of my grandparents Gertrude and Sidney Ransom who struggled with supressed enmity the onslaughts of a struggling civilization

Prologue

"Between two worlds Life hovers like a star,
Twixt Night and Morn, upon the horizon's
*   merge.*
How little do we know that which we are!
How less what we may be!"

Lord Byron

Chapter One

It was the season of torrential rains, uncertainties and fears as great investment crops were threatened with disaster. Henry Pearson frantically called together all his hands to plan for the impending storm that could destroy his five hundred acres of wheat crop.

The Pearsons reigned at the top of the landed gentry in Forrestville, Virginia, a large farm area in Lancaster County. Their position was secured by many generations of land acquisition and wealth.

Henry III had inherited the responsibility for perpetuating the legacy of great land owners. He ascended to the position of power with great ease, since he was the only male and his two sisters had chosen to live in the North.

After his graduation from the famed Lee and Washington University, Henry had entered the aristocratic hierarchy with the ease of a young king ascending to the throne. Five years prior to his death, his father, Henry Pearson II, had drilled his son in the rights and responsibilities of his leadership role as head of the largest land possession in the county.

Henry's knowledge and training for such a role, along with his strong commitment to his heritage, had sustained him through many onslaughts of nature that are inherent in farming. The impending disaster to his largest wheat crop caused him overwhelming anxiety since there was so little time to prepare or gather his forces, but he summoned all the fortitude of his breeding.

According to nature's signals—and frequent weather reports—he would have to work around the clock to save the crop. Word went out to all parts of the county, to all farmers large or small, for help. They responded in mass to the call, compelled by their unwritten code to help each other in trouble. The major landowners joined with Henry in a frantic effort to plan strategy.

The wheat was cut, tied and stacked, but with the forecast of great winds and rain, it would have to be threshed immediately or be lost. They called in all available threshers; only a few privately owned ones were not in use during this season.

Henry concluded he would have to work with fewer machines, but more men and throughout the night to save most of his crop. Members of the Land Gentry Council agreed to call in all their field hands to assist his workers.

The issue of pay for the workers emerged and became a flaming issue. Ten cents an hour was the going rate, but Henry was willing to pay them more in this case.

"I'll give them more if they work all night," Henry said, enraged by the other land owners' priorities. "They deserve more, by God, so much is at stake here. This is no time to discuss hourly pay; all hell is about to break loose out there."

"I'll be damned if you will, Henry," bellowed John Lawson, the second-largest land owner in the county. "If you do, I'll not release any of my workers to help you. If you pay them more now, they'll expect the same pay when this is over, and the rest of us won't stand for that."

Henry's uncle, the only doctor in Forrestville and a first-rate hereditary farmer, spoke up.

"If we pay them more now, Henry, how will we be able to get them back to their regular pay. I say we pay them the same ten cents an hour no matter when they work. I fail to see why you should pay them any more. Most of these blacks live on our land almost free, and others still owe us for the land they're supposed to be buying. They owe us just for keeping them alive."

"But Uncle Boyd, this is an unusual situation, a critical one, and we are wasting valuable time arguing."

"No matter what the situation, Henry, the pay remains the same," replied his uncle emphatically.

"But suppose they don't accept such pay since it's their own time?" asked Henry.

"They'll have to accept it. What else can they do? Where else can they go? They'll do what we tell them to do and that settles it. Let's get to work," commanded John Lawson.

Henry conceded to the regular hourly pay of ten cents no matter how long they worked or under what conditions. He felt uncomfortable about the decision, but what could he do; his major crop was at stake.

The Council members departed hurriedly with promises to join forces with all their field hands at midnight. They all expressed an exalted power over the Negro workers but were a bit shaken by the power of nature. They were the land aristocracy who must prevail—it was their proclaimed right.

3

Henry went to the kitchen to give Ada instructions for food and coffee through the night. Ada was his housekeeper and, along with her husband Alexander, had helped him since he had taken over after his father's death.

They had worked for the Pearson family off and on for many years. They always came to help when there was a special need. Since Alexander had turned his farm over to his sons, he and Ada had agreed to work for Henry until he was established and found more permanent help.

Henry acknowledged the suddenness and extent of his request, but assured Ada that the women from the Council members' homes would come to help her.

The night was filled with frantic excitement and glowing torches by which hundreds of workers labored, feeding the threshers, loading the wheat, and hauling it to storage to protect it from the hurricane winds and heavy rains expected.

The women served food and coffee all through the night; the workers were relentless in their efforts to save the crop. Henry rode the field, keeping watch from horseback.

Amid the torch lights, Henry saw an unfamiliar young woman's face. She was serving coffee without anything on her glistening auburn hair. Even in the torch light he could see she was beautiful, but his mind was forced to deal with more relevant matters.

Henry continued circling the field on his horse to assure himself that everything possible was being done. Heavy clouds rolled in, darkening the night and making it almost impossible to see. He ordered additional torches to brighten the field more so work could continue until completed.

He ordered more coffee and sandwiches for the men. Mary, Ada's granddaughter, returned to the field driving a buggy filled with food and coffee. She stopped at the edge of the field where the men were loading sacks of wheat on trucks and wagons bound for the Pearson Mill.

Henry rode up and asked for coffee; Mary handed it to him without speaking. The torch light flashed across her face. It was the same face he'd seen earlier, but he did not recognize her.

"Who are you? I haven't seen you before."

"My name is Mary. I am Ada's granddaughter. She asked me to help."

Again he was struck by the presence of this girl silhouetted by the torch light and the glistening night. He quickly gave her an order.

"Drive the wagon around the edge of the field and stop where the men can easily reach you. Join the other women when you've made a complete circle, then in a couple of hours start again. Keep it up until everything is finished here. Just follow the torch lights around the field and the men will find you." Then he galloped away like a dark knight to battle.

Mary drove slowly around the edge of the field filled with excitement of the night and the sight of black and white men working together. The only obvious difference was that the Negro men were half clad, while the whites wore raincoats. She thought how sore they would be when the wheat chaff whelped their skin, leaving it sore and bleeding.

Pouring coffee for the black men loading the heavy sacks of wheat on the wagons and trucks, she couldn't help but admire them. Their unshirted bodies glistened from the rain, and they seemed to work with a quiet, noble strength.

Her eyes caught casual glimpses of Henry as he rode in and out of the flickering torch lights like a great general commanding his troops. Against the background of the night, he projected an image of a knight from his high position on the stallion.

She quickly dismissed her vision of him and returned to the house with the other women for more food.

Back in the kitchen Mary said, "Grandma, all the food is gone. We have to fix more. The men are so hungry they are eating it faster than we can get to all of them. Looks like this night will never end. I don't see how they can stand it."

"All right, chile, we'll fix more. I sure am glad you are here to help. Don't know what I'd a'done without your young legs and mind," Ada replied, giving the other women instructions to prepare more food.

The siege continued until morning when Henry announced that most of the wheat had been saved and was safely stored in his mill.

He expressed his gratitude to his neighbors, friends and hired hands—his own and those from other farms. He instructed his foreman to pay off the men and to see that they got rides home. The convoy of trucks, wagons, carts and threshers moved slowly onto the road in the misty morning rain, filled with exhausted men.

It was like a victorious battle; the soldiers were leaving the battlefield weary but proud, leaving only the residue what was.

Returning to the house, Henry told Ada that she and Alexander could leave and not come back until the next day. He went to his study, took a strong drink of his favorite bourbon, slumped in his easy chair and surrendered to exhaustion.

When Ada returned the next morning, Henry asked her about Mary. "Ada, I don't remember your granddaughter. I really didn't know you had one."

"She lives in Baltimore with her mother, my daughter. She spent more of her summers here with me when she was a young child. She came to stay with me so she can go to Virginia State College; it's cheaper if she's from Virginia."

"Will she be working this summer, and where?" Henry asked, genuinely interested.

"I'd hoped she'd get to work here. We sure could use some help this summer, 'specially with your sisters coming. Alexander and me is gettin' old and Mary could be mighty helpful. She sure could use the money for school."

"Sure, Ada, I guess you could use the help. It'll be nice having her here." He turned and left without further comment.

Ada told Mary that night that she would be working with her for the summer.

"It's sure a good thing, Mary, that you got a chance to earn a little money to help with your schooling. Your mother sure can't do it by herself. She's had it pretty hard since your poor father died. We all want you to go to that college; we's so proud of you."

"I know. Grandmother, you and Grandpa have been so good to us. Mother and I couldn't have made it without your help. I am glad to have the job for the summer; my scholarship doesn't cover everything." Mary kissed her grandmother good night.

The next morning Mary joined her grandparents, assuming her duties under Ada's supervision at the Pearson estate, that in previous years had been a great plantation.

She quietly entered the breakfast room with Henry's breakfast. He was reading the paper, so she quickly placed the food on the table, trying not to disturb him.

He lifted his head slightly and got a glimpse of Mary as she was leaving.

"Who are you?" he asked, not recognizing her in her new role and dress.

"It's Mary, Mr. Henry."

"Mary who?" he asked, appearing confused.

7

"Don't you remember, Mr Henry? I'm Ada's granddaughter."

"Oh, yes, I remember now. I am sorry I forgot. So much has happened. Everything is fine. Thank you for bringing my breakfast."

"Yes, sir," she said and hurried from the room.

The rains continued and Henry remained in the house attending to his paperwork and listening to the silence of the big house that only came alive once a year when his sisters visited. The days drifted in dull dreariness and boredom and brought loneliness to the surface.

A sharp bolt of lightning pierced the darkness of Henry's bedroom. He awakened with a sudden jolt and sat straight up in his massive four-poster bed surrounded by rural darkness. The persistent rain made him feel a deep loneliness inside of him that would not let him sleep.

Since the death of his parents and his sisters' migration to the North, he had become absorbed in running the estate. Such responsibilities kept his days full, and at night he willingly conceded. This had become his routine since taking over.

He was feset and annoyed by the empty feeling that was invading his body. He had never felt so lonely or isolated before tonight. Maybe it's the rain making everything desolate, he thought.

He always had lots of friends in school and at home, especially young women like Martha Lawson, whom he had been seeing since his return home. Her father was the next biggest land owner in Forrestville and had been a close friend of his father's. He liked Martha and saw her often. He took her to all the social occasions. But even though her parents expected it, the relationship had not progressed to the point of marriage.

John Lawson, her father, had often mentioned

that his marriage to Martha would unite two of the most powerful families in the county, and he wanted his legacy and lineage continued. Henry knew this was expected of him and had no real opposition to it or to Martha, who was willing.

She was lovely, with long blonde hair, charm and grace. She was well educated and thoroughly understood the responsibilities of ruling land gentry. It was obvious to him, and to others, that she loved him.

He had felt for some time that he should marry her. There was no one he cared for more than Martha. He lay in the darkness assessing all of her fine qualities, qualities that gave him a quiet sense of security for his future family and its continuation. Yet thinking of her didn't fill the empty hollowness inside him, and the feeling had often persisted even in their most intimate moments. His inexplicable reluctance to propose was like being in limbo, not really propelled in any direction, just waiting.

Henry continued to lie awake in the darkness listening to the monotonous rhythm of the rain, wrapped in the intimacy of his thoughts and feelings. He could not sleep; there seemed to be a disturbing efficacy in the atmosphere: in his house and in his life. His body shivered with unruly desires and a need for passionate closeness.

The next day Henry called Martha and they made plans to spend the day together at a resort thirty miles away. He wanted to escape the feelings of the night before and yearned for an action-filled day. They spent long, leisurely hours of undisturbed intimacy that urged Henry to make it permanent. During the ride home they talked of the fun they would have when his sisters came home. He was filled with the joy of the moment but was unable to make the commitment the day warranted. Martha was happy with the certainty of what would follow. Henry slept deeply that night, satisfied that Martha was the one for him.

The morning sunlight drifted into his room, gently awakening Henry. He was filled with new energy for his day's plans.

With the appetite of a starving man, he headed for the kitchen to give Ada his breakfast order.

"Ada, I am starving. Fix me hot biscuits, ham, eggs, lots of hash browns and coffee. Got a lot to do before my sisters come."

"Yes, Mister Henry, Mary's gonna be a help in getting the house readied, since it ain't been used like this in a year."

"Ada, I think Miss Susan and Miss Elizabeth will be here for a couple of weeks. That means this house will come alive again with parties and lots of people. It's good you have Mary to help you. It's just good to have a young person around."

"I'll have Mary bring your breakfast, Mr. Henry."

"Ada, have Alexander saddle my horse. I want to check the fields to see what damage the storms did."

"Your breakfast will be ready in no time." She began preparing his requests, glad to see him in good spirits again.

Mary entered the brightly colored breakfast room with Henry's food. She was dressed in a clorox-white dress, her straight dark hair braided across the top of her head. It was neat, efficient and geared for work. Her light, creamy skin glistened with youthful freshness. She quietly placed the food on the table, trying not to disturb Henry, who was so absorbed in his newspaper that he didn't look up.

"Mister Henry, here's your breakfast. If you need any more, I'll be in the kitchen. I hope everything is the way you want it." She spoke in a soft, quiet, gentle manner and turned to leave the room.

Henry looked up, startled by Mary's presence.

She had spoken so softly he had not heard her. He unconsciously began to scrutinize her, aware of her quiet but disturbing demeanor.

Awkwardly he said, "You are Mary, aren't you? Ada's granddaughter? There's been so much confusion here for the past few days I hardly recognized you." He said it almost apologetically and a sudden need to know more about her emerged.

"How old are you, Mary?"

"I am eighteen," she answered and eased closer to the door.

"Don't rush away, Mary. I'd like to know more about you." He continued talking while he ate breakfast, and she busied herself in the room until he was finished.

"Will there be anything else, Mister Henry?"

"No, Mary, that's enough. Tell Ada I enjoyed it."

Henry was impressed by this efficient, self-assured and beautiful girl, but her presence made him strangely uncomfortable.

"Mary, I am glad you are staying on this summer. Your grandmother can really use you. I had offered to hire someone to help her, but she refused. She's getting on in age and my sisters like entertaining while they are home. It's only once a year, but it's hectic."

"Grandma only wants me to help her this summer, then I'll be going to college in the fall. She feels I could use the extra money," she replied without looking at him. "If you are finished, Mr. Henry, I'll clear the table and help Grandma in the kitchen." She tried not to show how anxious she was to leave the room.

"That'll be all, Mary. Thank you. I'll be working in my study the rest of the day; you can bring my lunch there."

"Yes, Mr. Henry." She quickly left the room.

"Mary, chile, what took you so long?" Ada asked

anxiously. "Was everything alright? I was getting worried. I figured you'd be coming right back."

"Everything was fine, Grandma. Mr. Henry just wanted to talk, so I straightened up the room while he talked. He seems like a lonely man."

"That's fine, chile," Ada replied. "There's just so much to be done before his sisters come home. They is very particular and likes lots of parties with plenty of people. I am sure glad you are here. I don't think your grandfather and me could handle it by ourselves. It jest gets harder each year and I don't feel up to it much more. I jest want to hold on long enough for you to finish college. That's the most important thing in my life now, then I'll rest in peace," Ada said, wearily wiping the sweat from her wrinkling skin with her apron.

As the day unfolded many arduous tasks arose that were necessary in preparing the large, unused house for guests. Ada assigned Mary to serving all Henry's meals, which she accepted obediently.

Mary's multiple racial mix of white, Indian and Negro, indigenous to Virginia, made her an exceptional beauty. Her long, dark hair, light creamy skin, greenish-blue eyes, high cheekbones, delicately-shaped nose and full, voluptuous mouth produced nature's beautiful combination.

The selective breeding process used in slavery had created a different kind of Negro called W.I.N.s: White, Indian and Negro. This genetic mixture made them distinguishable from others. Although they were still Negroes, this distinction sometimes created conflicts between the groups.

A difference of roles during the days of slavery reinforced these barriers. W.I.N.s had always accepted their role as house servants with a certain dignity and acculturation that distinguished them from those who worked in the fields. Some were direct descendants of

12

the masters during slavery and many were free-born. They learned to emulate the dress and manner, selection and preparation of food and home furnishings of their masters from working in the house. This included a strong desire for education and land ownership.

The Negro community became divided by color; distrust, hate, envy and jealousy surfaced that would last for many generations.

Ada's family and others like them accepted both their distinction and its negative aspect. As a minority of a minority, they faced a double racial impact.

Ada and Alexander were very active in the church, even taking leadership roles, and reared their children to do the same. She was active with the House of Ruth and Eastern Star and he with the Masons. The word "black," in reference to people, was never permitted to be used by any member of the family, even when derogatory names such as "half-white," "high-yellow" and "half-breed" were hurled at the children in school.

Mary worked endlessly with her grandparents in preparing the house for the expected visitors and their social activities. They pursued the routine tasks of polishing the imported silver, getting out the china and fine linens. They planned menus for each occasion and selected food and wines, with all conversation geared to the purpose at hand.

Mary continued to serve Henry his meals since he ate alone. Her constant presence became accepted by him and even expected. He had begun to look forward with anticipation to her quiet, pleasant service and conversation.

He enjoyed talking with her, even though she said very little, just enough to be courteous and maintain her position with dignity. Mary's presence eliminated his bachelor isolation, but his loneliness returned at night when she and her grandparents had gone.

Henry found himself excited and looking forward to the social activities that always accompanied his sisters' visits. In the past he had only endured them because it was a tradition of the family. It helped to keep the family ties strong and kept his sisters informed about their their shared inheritance, which included substantial financial benefits that enabled them to maintain their social status in Boston society.

The ten-hour day that Mary and her grandparents had worked provided satisfying results: the house was invitingly ready for all occasions. Henry gave his glowing approval and the scheduled arrival of his sisters was heartily welcomed.

Chapter Two

The early morning dew glistened on the green lawn and the sun signaled all to rise. Henry thought, it's a good day, so much to do. He had to drive to Richmond to pick up his sisters at the train station, an all-day trip he did not really want to make alone.

Maybe Alexander could go and help him drive, he thought, and help with the luggage that was usually quite prolific. His sisters always came prepared for all occasions, even unplanned ones.

Ada, Alexander and Mary arrived about six in the morning driving their horse and buggy. They saved their second-hand Model T Ford for special occasions, and the distance from their house to his was only about five miles. They liked to save gas whenever possible, since it was a luxury for them.

Henry entered the kitchen where the three were busy preparing the day's schedule.

"Good morning," he said with a boyish excitement seldom seen so early in the morning. "Oh,

Alexander, I want you to help me drive to Richmond today to pick up Miss Susan and Miss Elizabeth. I am sure Ada and Mary can manage without you and I will need help with the driving and the heavy luggage. We'll leave as soon as I have had breakfast. Ada, I want you to pack a nice lunch for us. In order to save time, I don't think I'll stop too long to eat," he continued.

Ada knew quite well that the lunch was for Alexander's sake since there was no place for Negroes to eat but plenty of fine places for whites to eat, especially a man like Mister Henry who was known and respected throughout the state of Virginia.

"Sure will, Mister Henry. I'll get started on it as soon as I am done with your breakfast. You jest go on in the breakfast room and Mary'll be right there. Y'all sure got a fine day for a ride to Richmond—clear and sunny weather," she continued, feeling Henry's enthusiasm.

Alexander was so excited that he could hardly contain it. A trip to a big city like Richmond was something he always looked forward to. He had been there only twice, both times with Henry, and looked forward to such trips. He and Ada had always planned to go to Baltimore to see their daughter but never found the time, the money, or the occasion.

At dusk the weary travelers returned, pulling into the driveway of the Pearson colonial mansion. The top of the car was loaded with luggage and so was the trunk. Henry's sisters rushed anxiously to the house as if it were their first time.

Henry turned to give Alexander a quick order, "Carry in the luggage. Put Miss Elizabeth's in her room and the same for Miss Susan. I'll see you inside a little later."

"This place looks the same. It's such a good feel-

16

ing not to have to face so many changes when you come home. Henry," continued Elizabeth, the older of his two sisters, "you have just done wonders here, running the farm, the mill, the cannery and this big house."

They continued to walk around the house, like children seeking assurance that all was the same as when they were growing up, that the love and security their home offered them then was still there.

They were once again bound closely by their memories and surrendered to the quiet nostalgia that filled them. Entering the beautifully landscaped garden, they stopped to admire the breathtaking array of flowers. The gardens bore a definite similarity to the Roman models that had inspired their mother on her visit to Italy.

"Let's sit here for awhile and talk," suggested Susan. "There are just so many things I want to say to you, Henry." Elizabeth and Henry willingly agreed, since daylight was slowly surrendering to the force of darkness. They sat on the beautiful, white marble garden bench where they could enjoy the extensive landscape colorfully decorated by the setting sun.

"Henry," remarked Susan in her warm and loving tone, "this house needs a woman. Don't you think it's time you married and had a family who could enjoy the great joys found here. You've been alone too long and this house needs a mistress, one who fits in with our traditions and who is capable of carrying them on."

"I think we'd better go inside. Ada has dinner ready and I am sure you'll want to freshen up first. We've time to talk later; there's so much that needs to be said."

As they entered the house, Ada came to the massive reception hall and greeted them, warmly yet tactfully reserved. "Oh, Miss Elizabeth, Miss Susan, I am just so glad to see you again. It seems so long since you been home."

They both put their arms around Ada and embraced her, placing loving kisses on her cheeks.

"My, Ada, you haven't changed. You *make* my homecomings. I always expect to see you. It wouldn't be home without you and Alexander," said Elizabeth, holding Ada at arms' length and looking endearingly at her aging figure.

"That goes for me too, Ada. You've been a part of our lives for so long, you are like one of the family," added Susan.

"Well, dinner is ready in the main dining room when you is ready. It's a real special dinner with all y'alls favorite dishes, fixed jest the way you always liked 'em. Jest call me when you is ready," Ada said in a joyous but almost tearful tone as she left them.

"It's going to be great to eat Ada's good cooking again. It was on my mind during the whole trip home," remarked Elizabeth as they ascended the graceful winding stairway. "See you later, Henry," she yelled to her brother as they disappeared into their respective rooms.

The dining room appeared classically transformed with Florentine silver, German stem crystal and Wedgewood china gracing the Chippendale table. There was an atmosphere of magic liveliness in the house that hadn't been felt for several years.

Henry arrived first to choose the wine and make a final check with Ada. He was a striking figure in his all-white suit. He seldom wore the suit, but he liked the master-of-the-house feeling it gave him. His imposing six-foot-two figure topped by sun-tinted, reddish brown hair was the epitome of Southern aristocracy. Every Southern belle in the state wanted the singular honor of being Mrs. Henry Pearson and being mistress of the historic mansion.

18

Susan and Elizabeth were glowing in their soft-flowing chiffon dresses as they seated themselves at the table, with Henry at the head. They loved their brother, and their admiration of him carried a deep, profound respect. They had shared so many private dreams, plans, hopes and problems with him that a bond had grown between them which time and distance had not, could not, diminish.

"This is just like old times when Mama and Papa were living," Susan said in an eager tone of voice that reflected her happy childhood. "It gives me a warm sense of security to be among the exquisite and classic memories that this place invokes in me."

"Susan, there is not that much difference between the things here and the things we have in Boston. Why so much elation? You grew up with all this." Elizabeth questioned.

"That's true," Susan said, "but there are so many changes taking place in the South, I feel reassured when nothing has changed here."

"Finish your champagne, girls. Ada's waiting to serve her special dinner. We can reminisce later," Henry said as he rang for dinner.

Mary entered the room first to serve the soup. Conversation came to an untimely halt as all eyes tried to absorb this tall, slender young woman dressed in white, her long dark hair pulled tightly to the back in a neat bun, and her shining olive skin glowing without makeup. Even Henry seemed shocked at her presence, almost stunned. As if it were the first time he had seen her.

He quickly, and almost awkwardly, began to explain Mary's presence. "This is Mary, Ada's granddaughter who's visiting her for the summer. Mary, these are my sisters, Elizabeth and Susan."

"Hello, Mary. It's nice to have you," Elizabeth said courteously.

"Why haven't we seen you here before, Mary?" asked Susan. "I don't remember Ada telling us about you."

Henry began to eat, wondering about the feelings that seeing Mary tonight had caused in him, but feeling obligated to further explain her sudden appearance.

"Mary is planning to go to Virginia State College here in the fall, and Ada hasn't been too well lately. So I agreed that Mary could help her. Ada is aging, and running this house and taking care of me is a lot for her," Henry said apologetically, not knowing why since everything he said was the truth.

"God, she is beautiful. She looks much different from most Negro women around here," remarked Susan.

"You remember Ada's daughter Rachel who married and moved to Baltimore. That's Mary's mother. If you girls can remember, Ada used to be a very attractive woman when we were children, if we ever had time to notice her," Henry remarked as memories of their childhood began to invade his thoughts.

Mary and Alexander continued serving the other courses in their quiet, friendly manner.

"Miss Elizabeth and Miss Susan, Ada fixed all your favorite dishes, and everything was grown right here on your land. Even the wine and the brandy was made here," stated Alexander proudly.

"Alexander, you tell Ada I'll be in to see her after dinner. I think we should have a little chat like old times," Elizabeth said as she dismissed him.

The dinner conversation was quickly directed toward Henry as the sisters began to quiz him about his personal life.

Realizing the intimacy of the forthcoming discussion, Henry suggested they have coffee in the library for more privacy.

In the dimly lit library the three seated themselves in dark leather chairs grouped for closeness and intimate conversation.

"Henry, you are twenty-five years old. There is so much living for you here. This house was built and furnished for gracious living, and you need a wife and family to share it with you. It's been three years since Papa died. Your new life must begin soon," Elizabeth stated in a motherly manner.

"You are right, Elizabeth, but it has taken me this long to adjust to running a farm, a mill and a cannery. I have had little time for myself, let along courting. Things will work out in time, no need to rush them. Don't forget, you two, how much you look forward to your share of the profits. If I marry things might change," Henry replied, trying not to show his irritation at their invasion of his private life.

"What about Martha Lawson? You two have always liked each other ever since we were children. Our families always figured that you would marry," Susan remarked knowingly, as if the matter was settled. She got up and poured a glass of the family's homemade peach brandy.

"We have planned several parties during our visit, and we always include the Lawsons. Let's make it a real celebration this year, Henry—why don't you and Martha announce your engagement. This is a lonely life for a man like you. I really don't think it's healthy to live alone," Elizabeth said with deep compassion and concern for her handsome brother.

"You need sons. You are the only male left to carry on the Pearson name," Susan picked up the conversation. "One should never live alone, especially when every eligible woman in this county would give anything and everything to be your wife. Youth is so short lived. The vital signs disappear quickly."

"You are both right in everything you say, but I

21

have my own plans," Henry replied. "Maybe I don't need to move as fast as you two did. You knew what you wanted and didn't have to concern yourselves with the family heritage and our status in the community. These are things I must think about. When I am sure Martha is the right one—and I really think she is—we will get married. So why don't you two discuss your social plans. You should also discuss them with Ada in the morning, by the way. We'll talk more about business matters later. Actually, a good night's sleep is what we need now." Henry kissed them good night and went to his room.

Henry was happy for the solitude of his room. He needed to deal with his feelings without intrusion. He had been uncomfortable, unreasonably so, when Mary had entered the dining room. Her presence disturbed his total being like no other woman's did, even those he had had passionate sex with in college. For Martha he had a comfortable love without excitement or fire.

He needed to make a final decision about marrying Martha. Perhaps that would make him safe from these feelings. Mary's quiet, gentle beauty and defiant manner had invaded an area of his feelings that had never been touched before. He didn't understand it, and it annoyed him.

"This is stupid," he thought to himself. "Maybe I have been alone too long. Loneliness is like a child born of unwed desires." Having made his decision to marry Martha, he retired—not to sleep, not to dream, just to drift through the darkness in rigid stillness.

Susan and Elizabeth entered the breakfast room eager to begin their plans for the big party. Ada brought them breakfast and arranged it buffet style. "Good morning, Miss Elizabeth and Miss Susan. I sure hope everything was to your satisfaction last night. I was feeling kinda poorly; I ain't been feeling well for some time now. I hope Mary done a good job. She is jest learning and she tries hard."

"Everything was wonderful, Ada," Elizabeth assured her. "You have done a remarkable job keeping this house in such excellent shape. But Miss Susan and I are planning a pretty large party here this week, so you may need some extra help. Since our time here is a little shorter this year we'll have to work fast. We will plan it out this morning and talk with you after that."

"Good morning girls; it's a marvelous day for horseback riding. I have just finished checking the stables and Jim says the horses are primed for riding." Henry made the statement in the form of an invitation. He collected his breakfast and joined his sisters in the cheerful breakfast room where bright rays of sunlight flowed through ruffled white curtains.

"We'll go later. Elizabeth and I must make plans for the party and that will probably take the entire morning. There are a few people I would especially like to see, like one old beau and the wife I have never seen, just to compare. I think you understand about female curiosity," responded Susan in a flirtatious tone.

"Ladies, I surrender the house to you. I plan to be out all day. I have to go to the mill and the cannery and check with John about paying the seasonal pickers. I'll be back for dinner," Henry said, finishing his coffee on the way out of the room.

Henry knew that his day had to be especially consuming physically and emotionally. After last night he felt safer away from the house.

At the end of the day, after checking his businesses and being satisfied that all was going well, he started home. But suddenly he changed his mind and

23

headed for Martha's house.

Martha greeted him in her usual charming manner but could not conceal her surprise.

"Henry, please come in. I am so happy to see you—a little surprised, but happy," she kissed him lovingly and he eagerly responded, something he had never done before.

"We are having dinner. Come join us. Mama and Daddy will be so glad to see you," she continued talking as they entered the spacious dining room. John Lawson rose to greet them with outstretched hands and a beaming smile.

"Henry, my boy, come in and join us. This is a pleasant surprise. We were just commenting on how long it's been since we have seen you." John spoke in a voice filled with a familial closeness.

"Good evening, Mrs. Lawson, I hope you've been well. I had intended to visit before now, but you know how busy this time of year is." Henry finished his greetings and sat down. Martha told the housekeeper to bring Henry some dinner.

As he ate he filled them in on the latest activities of the Pearson estate, "Elizabeth and Susan came home yesterday. I left them this morning planning their social schedule. I am sure they'll be contacting you; the girls always look forward to seeing all of you when they come home. Elizabeth, Susan, Martha, and I have done so many things together from childhood on that it will be good to be with each other once more." Henry suddenly stopped talking, sensing danger in his line of conversation.

"Henry," Martha suggested, "if you have finished your dinner, let's go out on the veranda. It's such a lovely night. Excuse us, Mother and Daddy. I want to talk with Henry."

She made a gesture to Henry and he followed her out into the night. "Henry, I don't know why you came tonight, but I have been wishing you would. We need to make some decisions about where our relationship is going. I have made it quite clear how I feel about you. We fit in every way, including between the sheets. I know you care about me, but you act like a frightened fox in the bushes, not knowing where to run, just hiding in the shadows." Martha was interrupted by Henry's bold, demanding kiss.

"You are right, Martha; it's time we did something and we are going to do it. After my sisters leave, we'll talk about it." Martha threw her arms around his neck, covering his face with hot, passionate kisses.

"Let's talk now, Henry. Why wait? Why are you delaying? I really don't think I can take much more of this waiting and wanting." Her passionate pleas were stopped by Henry's warm and gentle kiss.

"I really must go now, but we'll be together soon. You are a great woman, really great in every way." Henry left elated, but as he got nearer to his home, the euphoric feeling began to give way to demanding anxiety.

He went immediately to the privacy of his room to avoid prying conversation with his sisters. He wanted to be alone to nourish this emotional decision he had made about Martha.

The quiet morning was invaded by Elizabeth and Susan joyously revealing their party plans to Henry.

"We have agreed to have the party on Friday, since we must leave Sunday. It will be a small one this time because our visit is shorter," said Elizabeth with a sense of satisfaction and accomplishment.

"We'll have a small orchestra and we'll get more help for Ada," Susan continued. "She doesn't seem well, but her granddaughter Mary is a jewel. She and the other waiters we've hired will serve the hors d'oeuvres and cocktails. Uncle Boyd's cook will help prepare the food."

"By the way, Henry, we did not hear you come in last night. We wanted to talk with you. We were quite worried until we called Martha. She assured us you were all right and had just left her house," Elizabeth quizzed, not so subtly.

"Yes, it was quite late and I didn't feel much like talking. The day had been long and rather tiring. I stopped to see Martha to relax a bit before coming home," responded Henry as he continued his breakfast. "I am glad you two are throwing this party. It'll be good to have some excitement in the house after so much sober solitude."

"We'll be having lunch with Uncle Boyd today on his boat. Do you think you could join us, Henry? It'll be nice to glide down the Rappahannock River and watch the fishermen and crabbers at work." Susan invited, turning to Henry for his answer.

"No, I have quite a full schedule today; it's harvest time. So many things to check. But I'll see you at dinner. Oh, by the way, Martha invited us for dinner tomorrow evening about seven. I must go now; have fun." Henry left the house relieved not to be a part of their planning and subject to questions about Martha. They had always shared intimate things, but he wasn't ready to talk about Martha or any definite decisions concerning her.

Driving the long quiet road he became restless and uncertain, still struggling with numerous unanswered questions about his feelings.

*C*hapter
*T*hree

The room was filled with aristocratic socializing. Elizabeth and Susan reigned over the reception hall, a palatial room that struggled to maintain grandiose Southern tradition, as did its counterpart in many other mansions rebuilt or restored in the midst of unrelenting change.

"Elizabeth, have you visited George Washington's family home since you've been back?" asked Mrs. Martha Lawson, a proud Washington descendant whose estate was adjacent to the historical site.

"No, I haven't had the time this trip, and we're not going to be here as long as usual, I'm afraid. But I'm sure you keep it going. I often think of the days we spent there as volunteers. Have the tourists increased?" Elizabeth asked, trying to make conversation with the county dowager.

"You of all people, Elizabeth, should know how important this site is to the county since it's our greatest historical claim and an important part of our heritage. I do feel that you should stop in and see all the improvements we have made," replied Mrs. Lawson in an arrogant and demanding tone.

"Excuse me, Mrs. Lawson, I must mingle," Elizabeth said, seeing her uncle approaching. "Uncle Boyd," she greeted, relieved for the excuse to escape. "Susan and I had such a wonderful time with you and Aunt Ethel the other day on your boat. You and papa must have had many memorable times growing up here." Elizabeth put her arm around his neck and kissed him on the cheek.

"Yes, Elizabeth, your father and I had great times together. We were close brothers, since there were only two of us. The Pearson name will die if Henry doesn't have a son. I hope he'll marry young Martha. Their marriage would consolidate the two major families of this county. We have always had a heritage and she fits in."

"Uncle Boyd, I am amazed at your ability to serve as the only doctor in this area and run your farm, too. How do you manage?"

"I have a lot of good help; many of my workers have been with me for years so they are able to manage without me. That leaves me almost free to concentrate on my practice. I only do general medicine, but Dad always wanted a doctor-farmer in the family." He smiled and excused himself.

Susan was busy with the younger set, the offspring of the agrarian aristocracy. Their discussions centered on the social activities and fashions of the Northern elite. She told them of the great parties, cruises abroad, and the Paris fashions. They listened with mingled excitement and envy.

Martin Morris, the son of the county's legendary senator and the beau Susan had once thought she would marry, was in attendence. Young Morris had not recovered from the shock of Susan's surprising marriage to a young Bostonian of a prominent political family. On the rebound he had married Sarah Sommers, the daughter of a local merchant who sold farm machinery and implements. It was a lucrative marriage, however, that combined well with his father's political assistance.

"Tell me, Susan," he said, moving closer to her, "how is your husband?" He was not interested in the answer; he just wanted to talk to her and used words to justify his closeness.

"My husband is quite well and very busy with his law practice. He is planning to run for congress in a couple of years. His whole family has always been involved in politics. It is rather expected of him." Her tone was light, but she didn't move away from his close contact.

His wife, Sarah, tactfully invaded the conversation, "Susan, I hope you and Elizabeth will find time to visit us before you leave. I would like for you to see our two children. Come Martin, there are so many people here we must speak to." She guided him away quickly.

Martha and Henry circulated together, to the approval of their social peers. Their union would consolidate the two most powerful families in the county. To the Lawsons it was a long-hoped-for merger that would secure their future generations with power and position.

Alexander announced dinner and the guests moved eagerly into the dining room. Elizabeth invited them to be seated according to the place cards.

Susan had rearranged the cards to insure her seat next to Martin to see what effect she still had on him.

Henry took his rightful seat at the head with Martha on his right. Elizabeth placed herself in the mistress's position at the other end and directed the serving of the food.

Dinner conversation was dominated by the men. They shared information about farm-product prices, new machinery needed, labor costs, lost crops and finances.

Mary entered the room to assist in the serving. She moved with quiet assurance, a small white apron on a black uniform and a French-style white head-dress that accentuated her shiny dark hair and high-lighted her beautiful, light olive skin and classic features. All eyes turned in her direction.

The conversation stopped and everyone watched her as she moved around the table. She removed the dishes and left the room in the same quiet manner.

"Who is she, Henry?" they all asked in chorus.

"She is Ada's granddaughter who is helping out until she leaves in the fall for college. Ada needed additional help for the party." Henry was nervous and felt as if a threatening mist had invaded his mind. He began to struggle for appropriate words but gave up and said no more about Mary.

"She is a beautiful Negro, but she seems different. She almost looks white. Where has she been? I thought I knew all Ada's family," Mrs. Lawson asked with disturbing curiosity.

Elizabeth spoke up quickly, "She is Rachel's daughter. You remember her. Ada's daughter who married and moved to Baltimore quite a long time ago? Ada feels that Mary should have a state residency since she'll be going to the Virginia State College in the fall and it is cheaper for those who live in the state." She sighed and prayed for no more questions. She did not want to talk about Mary or think about her, so she changed the subject and maintained control of the conversation for the rest of the evening.

Henry invited the men to join him in the library for their brandy and coffee. As they entered the dark leathered room, they seated themselves with tradition-al familiarity. Alexander entered with coffee and brandy snifters, which he filled and served to each man. After completing the ritual he started to leave, but Henry interrupted his quiet exit.

"Thank you, Alexander. I'll ring if I need you again." After dismissing Alexander, he turned to his guests and took deliberate charge of all discussions and conversations.

In the living room the ladies eagerly asked ques-tions about Mary. Her presence seemed to have jolted them off their white aristocratic guard.

"Elizabeth, how can she go to college? Where did she finish high school?" asked Martha Lawson anx-iously.

"Most Northern city students attend high school free. We don't have a high school for Negroes in this county, so those who want more education must leave or pay to attend the private academy. I think that is why Mary's mother went to Baltimore, because of the price of the academy," Elizabeth answered in a super-ficially informed manner. "If Mary is registered as a state student, the college the tuition will be less. Between her parents and grandparents, they should manage all right."

"My daddy always said we didn't need a high school for Negroes since they had to work the farms," Martha said indifferently. "And anyway, they'd just have to leave school and go to work to help their fami-lies financially 'cause they are all so poor."

"She is unusually pretty," said Mrs. Lawson. "She has a different air about her, like she's been used to something. I'll bet Ada and Alexander have a hard time keeping those young Negro bucks away since they seem to start cohabitating so young." She reached for another glass of wine to cover the envy that might show on her face.

Ethel Pearson joined in with a solicitous air, "The only thing she can do is teach school, and there aren't that many jobs since there are so few high schools for Negroes, even in the cities. I know in Baltimore there is only one high school for Negroes. Ada has a cousin who teaches in the elementary school here. Like most of them it only has two rooms and two teachers. And most teachers stay forever since they can't marry."

Linda Morris spoke up with some degree of legislative knowledge since her father was a senator, "Father says this situation will soon be changing. The federal government is forcing counties like this one to build more schools, especially high schools for Negroes."

"I think that's great," replied Susan. "If we don't, according to my husband, we could have another Civil War. The people in the North are appalled at how Negroes are still treated in the South," she spoke the convictions of her husband, not her own.

"My husband, Senator Morris, agrees with this, but it means our taxes will be increased since most Negroes don't pay taxes."

"I think that's something for men to worry about, not us," said Susan nonchalantly. She'd lost interest in the subject and changed the conversation to clothes, parties, and travel.

"Morris, is there any truth in the rumor that a crab house is going to be built down in Merryneck?" asked Henry in a concerned tone.

"Yes, there is a company applying for such a permit, but I don't think it'll go through. So many people in this county would fight it."

"A crab house would mean disaster for people like us; we must band together and stop it," yelled a frightened John Lawson from across the room.

32

"Morris, you'll have to keep us informed about what's going on. Our future and the future of our children is at stake. I'll fight such an industry with everything I've got. If we want to stay alive we must fight."

Walter Carrington, the county's biggest banker, spoke, "You know that stretch of waterfront land in Merryneck where all the Negroes live in those broken-down shanties? It has been purchased by a Northerneck Company, but I am not sure what they plan to do with it. They financed it through another county bank, not mine."

"Who really owns that land now, Morris?" asked Henry as he kept the conversation on a topic that would consume their attention.

"If I recall correctly, there was confusion about ownership after the Civil War, but it is a part of the Cummings' old plantation. Many of the county's Negroes live and work there, fishing and oystering. There are very few other large farms in that section; it's the largest, although there is a scattering of small truck farms where some Negroes raise their own food. This is frightening. I'll run a search at the county court house as soon as I can," Morris assured them.

Boyd Pearson spoke up in an attempt to quiet their well-warranted fears: "Some of those people come to my office and they all seem destitute; I can't believe they own any land. The Negroes here in Forrestville seem to live much better, even on the barren land our fathers gave or sold them, but most of them will never be able to pay off the land on the wages we give them. I kinda feel that it's the same situation in Merryneck. We need to talk to the owner and persuade him not to sell. I'll begin asking more questions if anyone from that area comes to the office. They don't have a doctor in that godforsaken place."

He stopped when Henry interrupted. "Gentlemen, I share your concern, but I don't feel the need for alarm. You know times are changing, and we'll have to face it, make changes that fit the times even if that crab industry does not come here," he said. "Every year more young Negro men leave this county for the cities or for more progressive counties that have more industries. We'll have to invest in more farm machinery to work our crops. In some cases we have too many field hands doing the work that one machine could do."

Boyd Pearson, becoming panicked, interrupted him, "Most of my crops need pickers. They don't have any machine for crops that need hand-picking, and you all have those."

"Gentlemen," Henry stated firmly above the rising murmurs of agreement. "I think it's time we joined the ladies. There's no more we can do here tonight. We'll call a meeting for next week. Until then, I think we all need to do more research." Henry continued with polite conversation as he led the worried men out.

As they reached the living room, the unanimous greeting to their wives was, "Come ladies, it's time to go home."

Their exit was swift and confusing to the wives, but they followed without question.

Chapter Four

"Mary, next Sunday is the first day of revival meeting at the church. I guess we should go; no telling when I'll get there again with the canning to be done. Chile, I'm sure glad you is here this time 'cause I ain't feeling too well, and we'll have to cook lots of food to take. Mister Henry always lets me take a few days off for this, but your grandpapa will have to go to work, so he won't be much help to us." Ada patted Mary wearily on the shoulder as she spoke.

"Grandma, please don't try to do so much this year. I know how tired you are. I'll help you all I can, but there is so much to be done to feed all those people. They always come to your table, where they eat the most. I don't know how you can give away so much food," Mary said, looking at her dear and loving grandmother with deep concern.

"Honey, we been doing this for years. Can't stop now. Most of the people who've left here come back home for this week. We feed them because it's just so good to see them. They always give the church, we don't mind giving them a meal. Don't fret chile, I look forward to this every year, and I'll do it till I die. I sure hope your mama can get here; she ain't been for a long time." Ada continued talking as she rocked in her favorite rocking chair on the screened porch, that was built to join the house and the kitchen.

"I'll need four or five chickens, but I can't kill my laying hens. I need those eggs to trade for things at the store. I got a couple hams in the smokehouse; I'll jest use one of them. We'll pick lima beans and sweet corn from the garden for the succotash, and I'll take corn pudding, string beans, beets, maybe some fresh peas and stewed tomatoes. I'll make some rolls, sweet potato pies, and a big coconut cake. They always likes that. We's got three or four days and Grandpa can help us in the evening when he gets home. Don't worry, chile, we can do it. The Lord makes a way when you do His work," Ada assured her.

"Grandma, that's so much for us to do. Instead of washing and ironing the tablecloth and napkins too, can't we just use a nice, bright-white sheet for that outdoor wooden table?"

"Don't fret, Honey, we'll get it all done. There's lots of neighbors that don't carry a thing. They'll help us. Aunt Ruth's always ready to lend a hand. We'll ask her to come over and help you till I get home from Mr. Henry's.

"She likes you, and she jest lives across the field yonder. She's one of the hardest working women I've ever known. All her children are grown and gone and she's alone a lot. She's known by all as the Mother of Bungle Hook. I want you to go ask her tomorrow," Ada said as she left the porch to start her home chores.

When she went to Aunt Ruth's the next day, Mary would cross the open field on a path worn smooth and shiny by many years of family visiting, borrowing, and sharing. The path represented a bond born of necessity and survival, friendship that walking down the narrow road to the front of the house couldn't convey. The path led directly to each house's back door, the secure and welcome entrance.

Mary followed Ada into the kitchen to continue their current conversation. "Grandma, why is this place called Bungle Hook? That's a strange name. Where did it come from?" She sat at the kitchen table awaiting the answer.

"I ain't sure, chile. It was called that when I came here. Your grandpa had this land here when we got married, but I heard some tales. Most of what I know comes from your grandpa or Aunt Ruth. She was one of the first to settle in this godforsaken place. I hear tell this was used by free-born Negroes to hide Northern soldiers that came here during the Civil War. They bundled them up and hid them." She stopped talking as if struggling to remember things she had struggled hard to forget, as she began to recall stories handed down about slavery days.

"They says that the people used only the paths to go from house to house. It was a safer way to get food and water to the hiding soldiers. Nobody walked in the road, and still today you don't find people walking that road. We all use the paths through the woods or across the fields."

"Is that why we walk to Mrs. Smith's house all the time?" Mary questioned. "That sure is a well-used path. I don't think we have ever been down the lane that leads from the road."

"That's right, chile, and that's the way her children come over here. We all learnt them things from our parents. Things jest got handed down. We used to go through the woods to fetch water from the spring before we had a well. It seems we done spent most of our lives going through the woods. We go to the store that way too."

"But why, Grandma?" Mary asked, wanting to hear more.

"'Cause during that time it just wasn't safe to be on the roads. Black people did everything in secret ways, just to stay alive. Guess we still got lots of that in us today.

"Honey, let's don't talk no more 'bout it tonight. I got so much to get done before Sunday," Ada said wearily.

"I am sorry. I didn't mean to upset you," replied Mary, kissing her grandma on the cheek and hugging her with understanding.

"'Taint that, honey, it's just the going on—the going on when you don't feel you can go on, or know why you keep going on. But it's jest the going on that keeps a body going." Ada moved slowly into the house. No more words tonight.

That night Mary laid awake in her bed. She could hear her grandparents praying, always thanking God for their meager blessings. She thought to herself, this place, this Bungle Hook, is the key, the link for all the people in this section of the county, and it's filled with secrets, history, suppressed memories, and fear.

She finally slept a half-conscious sleep as the bright August moon sent its unshielded light through her window.

About five the next morning, Mary heard her grandparents going downstairs. She got up and washed at the washstand. Water was always put in the pitcher at night, and the towels were hung neatly on the rack over the stand. It was cold water, but it helped clear her head. She dressed, blew out the lamp, and joined them in the kitchen.

"Mary, you didn't have to get up so early. We don't need you to help at Mr. Pearson's today," Ada said. "I wants you to work with Aunt Ruth. We'll be off now; we'll be back after dinner. You know what needs to be done." Ada kissed Mary lovingly but quickly because Alexander was waiting in the buggy.

Mary knew the routine: she ate her breakfast, fed the hogs and watered them, fed the chickens and let the cow out into the pasture. Upstairs she made her bed, took the slop jars down to the woods and emptied them, washed them, carried them back upstairs. She collected the lamps, took them to the kitchen, washed the shades, refilled the lamps with oil, and took them back. Then she refilled the water pitchers and washed the bowls. She had drawn enough water from the well for the task, so she refilled the drinking water bucket that was kept on the screened porch between the kitchen and the house.

She carefully closed the house—no one locked their doors—and walked the path to Aunt Ruth's house. The early morning dew wet her tennis shoes, but it felt good. She had to move fast before the heat of noon.

Reaching the door of the back screened porch, she called, "Housekeepers." That's what everybody said before entering a house; she didn't know why.

Aunt Ruth came to the door. "Come in, chile. You sure are up early."

"Yes, ma'am. Grandma asks if you'll help me get the food ready for Sunday's revival meeting. She's got to work and we've only a few days to get it done."

"That woman sure fixes a lot of vittles for those folks to eat up. I stopped a long time ago. It got to be too much to do by myself, but I'll sure be glad to help Ada," she replied as she continued drinking her coffee.

"Want some coffee? I drinks four or five cups every morning. It gets me going. I keeps the pot on the stove all day. Now, before we gets movin' for your Grandma's, we got to go up to the store. I needs a few

39

things and we has to pick up the mail."

"I'll enjoy that, Aunt Ruth. It's been a long time since I been there."

"That's sure right, chile, you ain't been here for quite a spell. I hear you been working in the summers with your ma. Nothing's changed much here. We take the same back path through the woods we's always used. It's a shortcut, and it's a whole lot cooler than walking that main road. Come help me gather up some eggs to pay for my coffee and sugar."

Ruth continued talking as she picked up her egg basket and lined it with a clean kitchen towel.

Mary walked with her to the hen house and watched as she gathered up the eggs. checking each one to see if it was fresh and selecting only the large ones. They would bring a better price. Eggs were used like money to buy things. This barter system had been a custom as long as she could remember.

The main store was about three miles from Bungle Hook. It housed the post office for those whose mail wasn't delivered to their mail boxes. Only the well-to-do whites had boxes in front of their homes; no Negroes had them since they lived off the main roads.

As they began their walk to the store, Mary was overwhelmed by a desire to know more about her people and their community. What had always been taken for granted—quiet, peaceful, and secure—now seethed with the mystery of unanswered questions.

"Aunt Ruth, is everyone in Bungle Hook related?" Mary asked.

"Jest about. There's two families not related. There's the Woodsons—they were slaves and they was stuck back there in the woods. Nobody knows nothing about them. Then there's the Browns down this road. They came as pickers one year and stayed. Nobody knows much about them either, and they stay to themselves. The rest of the families are your relations."

"Why did they all just settle back here? They seem so cut off from the outside world," Mary commented as they walked.

"Chile, let's stop at the spring and get a nice cook drink and a rest 'fore we go on," Aunt Ruth replied wearily.

They both knelt down to drink from the fresh spring water and rested on a tree stump nearby.

"Mary, for many years we toted this water to the house every day. It was all the fresh water we had till we got wells. This spring has served us all. I used to carry two buckets at a time, sometimes three—one on my head. I am too old now. I'll be seventy-five soon, and all my ten children are grown and gone. I do manage to take care of myself, even though I am alone. It's been a hard life, but you learn to live the best way you can."

They began walking again and Mary renewed her questioning.

"Aunt Ruth, how long have you lived here? You seem to know more about this place than anyone else."

"This place was started for blacks who were not slaves, the free born. Some were given land and some bought it. Most of our folks were children of masters or mistresses. I guess we all come here so the whites wouldn't have to look at their sins."

"Why do you say that?"

"It's like this, Mary. My mother was a white woman. She was the daughter of a big plantation owner. My daddy was Indian. I was brought up by a black woman who used to work for them. When I was fifteen, I married an older man. They say my mother's folks died out quickly, and when she died, she left me all she owned. But the law said no black person could get the land, especially females. They took me to court a few times. There was a white man, a lawyer, who said he could help me, but he did no good. The Pearsons got all the land, and this little plot I live on now they sold us real cheap 'cause I was free."

"Is that what happened to my grandparents?"

"In a way. Your grandmother's mother was white, but she married a black man. There was some kinda law that said if your mother was white, you were born free. Your grandma'll tell you when we went to school we were called 'free niggers.' Them others seemed to jest hate us, so they tried to keep us apart. I guess that's one reason why we all live back here."

"What about Grandpa? All the people with his name are white."

"They all your cousins, chile. Most blacks and whites is related. His father was a Randall, a white man, and his mother was Negro and Indian. Most of our family is a mixture of white, Indian and Negro, but no matter what the mixture is, you still black. We done all learned to live with it; they jest want you to stay in you place."

"If that's true, Aunt Ruth, what about Mr. Watson's plantation on the water where our church holds the baptisms? How did he get that place if what you said is true."

"That's one of the unusual cases. His master didn't have a son by his wife, but he had him by a house slave. He had made good and sure that when he died, all his land would go to this chile who bore his name. But there no other 'round here like that."

They finally reached the little country store. "Marnin', Mr. Doggins," said Ruth.

"Morning, Ruth. How's you this hot day? What can I do for you?" he asked in his usual way.

"Here's my eggs. I only need a few things today. The eggs are fresh, jest gathered them this morning," Ruth replied.

"Who's chile is that with you? Don't 'member seeing her 'round here. Is she one of yours?"

"No, this is Ada's granddaughter. She's spending the summer here. I wants to get my mail while I am here."

"Sure, Ruth. Your children ain't doing much writing lately. There's a couple of letters and your Sears catalogue."

"Thanks, Mr. Doggins. We'll be gettin' on home now before the sun gets too hot," Ruth said over her shoulder as they left the place.

Walking behind the store to the long path back home, Mary turned and said, "Aunt Ruth, let me carry those packages for you. They look heavy."

"Thanks, chile, I could sure use some help. It gets harder for me each time. Sometimes I get a ride with your grandparents in the car. I am so glad they lives close to me," she replied gratefully. "So many of us depends on them to go places, even to church. I had to stop using my buggy after my horse was struck by lightning."

"Aunt Ruth, are you still midwifing? I bet you delivered everybody around here, white and black," Mary said, trying to keep the conversation going. It made the walk easier.

"Don't do it much anymore. Dr. Pearson takes care of most the whites. I still do for the Negroes. It don't cost them much 'cause some has no money. I been doing that work for over fifty years now. There's so many stories I could tell about these families around here, you just wouldn't believe."

"Go on, Aunt Ruth. You know so many interesting stories, more than anyone else. Our history only gets told verbally from one generation to another. Everything always seems so peaceful here, but there is so much behind and underneath that's worth knowing. I know life is hard, my mother told me she would

43

never live here, it was just too hard. That's why she left so young. She's worked so hard for me to go to college and have a better life. Not that she wants to forget where she came from. She loves her family very much. It hurts her not to see Grandma more than she does, but her work doesn't permit it."

"How's your ma been doing since your pa died? He was so young. It must be hard for the two of you."

"After Papa died, Mama got a live-in housekeeper's job and they let me live there too. They are rich and we don't want for much since we get our room and board. I have learned so much by living there. It's like the Pearson home.

"When I was fourteen, I had to stop coming here because my father died and I spent my summers helping my mother. The Houstons—that's the name of the family we work for—have a summer home in upstate New York. It is such a beautiful place. I'll miss going there. I'll probably work there in the summers to help pay some of my school expenses."

"Mary, you ain't working with her now. Don't you need the money?" Ruth asked.

"I do need the money, Aunt Ruth, but I came to Grandma's to earn state residency. The Houstons said it would be cheaper if I went to a college here," she explained as she shifted the shopping bag from one arm to the other.

"A college education costs so much. Several of my grandchildren are trying to go. I just wish I could help them. But you work hard, you'll make it. We is depending on you young ones to make it better," Ruth said as she looked for a place to sit down to rest her tired old feet. They both sat on a log and took off their shoes to relax a few minutes in the cool shade of the tall pines.

"Aunt Ruth, the white and black here are so closely bound by blood, but they act as if neither exists. We live in boundless secrecy that creates a wall around each race like the wall of China," Mary continued her observations with greater insight, and with a growing awareness of a perpetual facade.

"Many are bound, 'tis true, but some are closer than they know or will admit." As Ruth talked, waves of memories, unstirred for years, began forcing their way out.

"During my many years as a midwife, I saw and heard things that could never be told, but I am jest an old woman now. Guess nobody would even believe me. But, Mary, there's many blacks who are really white, and some is white, but is really black."

"What do you mean, Aunt Ruth? How could that be without it being known?" Mary asked curiously.

"Let's move on, chile, the sun is getting hot. We can talk as we walk. You see, during slavery or even after, the master would have a child by a house slave and one by his own wife. If the slave's child was fair enough, they would switch them. The slave wanted her child to grow up as belonging to the master, and she would take his. Slave families were often broken up and sold. They were sent to other parts of the country, never to see each other again. So the masters never knew. It wasn't anything for a slave woman to have a fair child since they were expected to bear masters' children. Nothing they could do about it.

"Sometimes the mistress would have a child that was not her husband's. The child would be given to a mammy to raise as her own. No one ever told for fear of their lives."

"So, the great wall of secrecy grew and grew and must remain with us forever," stated Mary quietly.

"Sometimes the mistress would have a child by a man slave. They would say that the child died, but most times if she didn't kill it, it was given to slaves to raise. The midwife was usually black and had to bear the burden of great secrecy," Ruth revealed, glad to talk about a situation to which she was born.

"Do such things go on now, Aunt Ruth?" asked Mary.

"Yes, but it's different in some ways. It depends on how rich the family is. They often pay black families to raise their bastards though they be white. Others may send them away to live with relatives." Nearing her house, just above the last hill, Ruth stopped talking of the past and faced the present and the tasks of the day which lay ahead.

"I enjoyed talking to you, Aunt Ruth, and I'll see you tomorrow when you come over. You have helped me to understand why things are the way they are and how my family fits into it all." Mary said goodbye and followed the path home. She stored the memories of their conversation for future use.

Chapter Five

The feudal lords gathered at the Lawson home to formulate an attack plan against the new industry invading their private domain.

"I have called you all here today to let you know the crucial situation we face," John Lawson said, introducing the topic for the group's meeting in a voice etched with panic. "We have found out that it's true: a crab house will be ready to open next summer, and you all know what that means to us as farmers. Now, just what in hell are we going to do about it?" he asked, sitting down almost exhausted.

"We just can't deal with this disastrous situation as feudal lords or slave masters," Henry said, taking the floor. "We must think like businessmen. I have as much to lose or more than some of you, but I am trying to find a reasonable way to deal with it."

"Henry, this is not a situation for reason but for action. This land has been in our families for hundreds of years. Land aristocrats are what we are and what we'll stay, no matter what it takes, even war," declared Boyd Pearson.

"Morris, just where will it be built, on whose land, and where is the money coming from?" asked Henry, trying to maintain a calm tone of voice.

"You know the Cummings plantation on the river? Well, the land has mostly been run by sharecroppers, and Cummings has an oyster house there, too. A cousin from another county is financing the project and it'll be a joint venture. There seems to be a great demand for crab meat, which will be their summer product. They also plan to increase the oyster production in the winter. This will give the workers year-round work. It's the biggest threat to the farmers in this county's history," said Morris, the county's representative in the State Senate, in a factual and unemotional voice.

"Hell, Morris, is there no legislation you can get through to stop it?" asked Lawson frantically.

"No, I am afraid there's nothing we can do in that area. The state feels the need for new industries and wants to develop markets for its natural resources. I am just as affected by this as the rest of you since I am one of this county's major farmers," he stated in a diplomatic voice touched with defeat.

"This means all our workers will be leaving to work there. How are we going to run a farm without workers? I know all those niggers will leave. But we can stop them," Lawson declared in a voice of authority.

"How do you plan to do that, John?" Henry asked. "You can't chain them anymore. We don't pay them enough to live. I don't have an answer, but I think we should talk to all our workers—white and black. They are both in the same situation."

"There's a possible solution to our problem," Lawson stated as if Henry hadn't spoken. "This is war, but not with guns or violence if possible. Most blacks live on our land, very few own homes or anything. They really belong to us. We can let them know that if they are thinking about leaving, their families will have no place to live. We can raise the rent; we can force them to pay the back rent they owe. If we all stick together, they'll realize they'll have no place to live and nothing to eat. What do you think of that plan, gentlemen?" he asked in his cold, calculating manner.

A spark of hope permeated the room and they began to respond with less despair.

"How do we execute this plan if we don't know who's leaving to work at the crab house? We could defeat our purpose if we move on this too soon," Henry said in a voice filled with great apprehension. "We could throw the whole county into panic and chaos."

"Henry, you were the one who said we must think like businessmen, and this is how business is done," Boyd Pearson interjected. "We must take the initiative and attack now, before the competition gets a stronghold, or you'll see thousands of acres of empty fields. I don't want to see what happened after the Civil War, when the carpetbaggers came, happen again. I am sure all your parents told you of their struggles to keep the land and restore our homes." Boyd Pearson forcefully stirred their memories, revitalizing their energy to fight and activating their need for power.

"If we begin this campaign now, by the time the crab house opens everyone will be too afraid to go there," Lawson said. "Most niggers are still filled with fear. They are conditioned to submit. Those who were able have already fled to the cities. Those who were afraid of change remain and can offer no resistance to this plan. No matter their struggles, they want to survive. This is what amazes me about these people. It's a great plan and I'm all for it. All of you who favor this plan raise your right hand." John Lawson happily surveyed the group's almost unanimous vote.

All eyes turned toward Henry Pearson in disbelief.

"Henry, you are the only one here who did not vote for this plan. Why not? You've got as much if not more to lose than most of us—your three thousand acres, your mill, your cannery. These people could leave you. Then what?" his uncle demanded.

"I am just not sure if it is the best way. We could increase their pay; they deserve it. To me that's the best way to hold faithful hard workers. I truly don't believe that fear of your kind will stop them. They live with it all the time; it's not new to them. They should be immune by now. This sounds so much like Klan action that it's frightening. I'll have to think about it," Henry answered cautiously.

"Man, we don't have time. Our lives and the future of our children are at stake," John Lawson screamed at Henry. "We must proceed while they don't suspect anything. You must be in this with us. You don't have a choice, and we don't intend to pay them niggers more money. If they had more money they'd get more independent. They are still here 'cause they don't know anything else, and they are bound by debt to all of us. It's either them or us, and it damn sure won't be us, I promise you. No matter what I have to do!"

"We'll put this plan in action as soon as the harvest is over. That must be taken care of first. Do we all agree?" asked Boyd Pearson.

"That'll give us about four more weeks," Lawson said. "In the meantime, formulate your individual attack plans and who's going to get the axe. This'll give them niggers something to think about all winter. Morris, find out what kinds of jobs they're gonna have, the pay, and about how many workers they're gonna need at that place. We want to know every move, every plan they have. By jove, we'll find a way to stop them, maybe before they even get started," the banker continued with a greater degree of confidence than earlier in the meeting. "I'll find out who's doing the construction work and where they're getting the boats and everything else they'll need for a big undertaking like that. Somebody is putting out a lot of money without checking on how folks like us feel about it. They just may be making the biggest mistake of their lives. We control everything and everybody in this county, and they'll have to come by us in some way.

"Men, let me warn you: don't discuss this with your women and don't talk about it around your house help. They listen to everything. Sometimes I think my housekeeper Tessie knows more about what goes on here than I do. That's why she's off tonight. There's no need to have the workers forewarned. That would just about ruin the whole plan."

The men reaffirmed their need for another meeting date and restated their individual tasks. Total secrecy about the attack was sworn by all, including Henry. John poured each a manly drink. As they drank, courage surged in them. Then they bade one another a cheerful good night.

The resounding voices of the men at the meeting plagued Henry the whole night. He couldn't sleep. He felt trapped, forced to face the reality of who he was and what was required of him to maintain his position. He had inherited his power, not worked or fought for it like the others. He felt a strong sense of guilt about his position in the group, not having shared their struggles, their fights, their fears, and the terrorizing decline of their power forced by time and change.

He knew he would remain a part of the land dynasty, but to what extent would he go to protect it?

He knew also that there was no way to stop economic and social evolution. It would take its natural course without concern for those it crushed. The process goes on. Those who have enough vision and wisdom to change with it can survive. All this he could see, but how could he adapt to these changes when bound so strongly by his culture, his heritage, his position, and his obligation to his friends.

He had become part of a decadent way of life by accepting all of its benefits without questioning how long it could prevail against the social evolution now taking place.

The question challenged every brain cell: how could he survive alone, yet how could he join in this plan with them? In either case he would lose something, but which would be the greater loss? Who would be his comrades to enter the new frontier with all its unknown vastness of possibilities, probabilities and problems? All the men he knew here were caught in the same trap of fighting to retain their proud place in the sun. Where could he turn and to whom?

He felt the great conflict of choice that the philosophers such as Voltaire, Rousso, Spinoza and others he had studied in college must have felt, those who had believed in the dignity of man. How could he reject such noble influences and remain a part of such a desperate plan, a plan to which he had made a superficial commitment. But he didn't want to hang, either alone or together with the others.

The crab house was not such an imposing industry, but it was a sign of the changes to come, changes that would rock the foundation of the South. The county's hold on their pre-Civil War culture was tenuous, too weak to sustain the high aspirations of the local land dynasties that were fighting for the survival of archaic racial laws.

Henry continued to contemplate his strategies.

He thought of how he would present the situation to his sisters without alarming them. He decided it would be best to write to them, and that would be his first task in the morning.

He welcomed the dawn and willed it to fade the midnight thoughts that had prevented sleep and left him completely drained.

Henry was in the kitchen fixing his coffee when Mary and Alexander arrived. "Where is Ada, Alexander?"

"She is feeling poorly this morning. She wore herself out cooking for the church revival meeting. I been telling her it's too much for her at her age. But Mary will help out here till she's better. I sure hope you don't mind, Mister Henry."

"How are you, Mary? It won't be long before you'll be leaving us for college." Henry felt the strong need to talk this morning. He enjoyed seeing Mary again and found many excuses to continue their conversation.

"Yes, Mister Henry, but I just hope Grandma is better before I go. She seems more than tired. She should see a doctor, Mister Henry. I am worried about her."

"I'll ask Uncle Boyd if he'll take a look at her. Can you get her to go to his office?"

"I am sure we can, Mister Henry. Thank you so much." She looked directly at him and smiled for the first time.

"I'll call him right away. You have a beautiful smile, Mary; you should do it more often. Don't fix much breakfast this morning. I don't feel like eating. I've got a lot on my mind." Henry left the room to call his uncle and he almost felt gratified to do this for her.

Mary entered the breakfast room with his coffee, juice and two hot corn muffins, his favorite.

"Mary, you and your grandfather can leave after

lunch and take your grandmother to Uncle Boyd's. You'll be back in time for dinner. There's not much to do and I'll be gone most of the day anyway." He looked directly at Mary, enjoying her quiet, classic, and compelling beauty.

"Thank you, Mister Henry. It's kind of you. We'll be back in time for dinner. Is there anything special you'd like to have?" she asked, smiling with gratitude and appreciation for his concern. A warmth filled the room, one of silent intimacy that existed without the clutter of words. Mary left him and returned to her duties feeling assured that all would be well.

Henry finished his breakfast more leisurely than expected, but the task before him reminded him of problems momentarily forgotten. He went into the library to write the necessary letters to his sisters. He stared at the blank stationery, pen in hand and mind searching for a way to tell a historical event in a few pages to two people whose lives were completely removed from the situation. How could he make them understand all the forces threatening their comfortable existence?

He struggled with the problem for an hour and then started writing. The resulting letters were sincere, honest, and compellingly brief, but they still took several hours to write. Relieved when he was finally done, Henry took the letters to the post office immediately and sent them registered mail.

Driving back he decided to take the side roads where his fields were being worked. He must talk to his foremen about rumors, rumbles and feelings about the forthcoming industry. He started first where the largest group of workers was picking tomatoes, one of his top cannery products. He felt sad for a moment. If he lost these workers, he would lose the cannery. He parked the car on the side of the road where he couldn't be seen and watched for a while. There were men, women, and children, even whole families, working the field that glowed with bright red tomatoes.

As he observed he became aware of the strength in these workers. Women young and old swung bushel baskets of tomatoes to their shoulders and carried them the full length of the long row to the road, where they were stacked for trucks to pick up.

The small children picked along with their parents and helped fill the baskets. They worked ten to twelve hours a day—bending, lifting, carrying heavy baskets for ten cents an hour, making enough money to survive, not to live. What machine could do this? he thought. He drove closer to the entrance where Jake, his foreman, was helping load the baskets on the trucks. He got out, walked over, and watched for a few minutes until Jake had a break.

"Morning, Jake. How are things going?" he asked as Jake stopped, but told the men to keep on.

"Morning, Mister Henry, I didn't know you'd be here today. Something wrong?"

"No, Jake, nothing's wrong. Just wanted to see how the last of the crop looked. Did we lose many this year?"

"No, Mister Pearson, no more than usual. I'd say it was a pretty good year, better than last year. The pickers seemed to work harder for some reason."

"Jake, are most of the workers from around this area? There seem to be many I don't recognize."

"Yes, many more workers are coming by truckloads from other sections of the county, further away than ever before. Work must be getting slow where they lives, but they are good workers. I think they must have a leader getting them together and bringing them here by truck, otherwise they couldn't come so far. They live too far away and they ain't got no other way to get here. The man that came to me to see if I needed more workers, he seems to be the leader. I

55

guess he goes around to all the farmers and finds work. Looks like he got himself a good business 'cause they gotta pay him something. He sure ain't doing it for free. But it's sure good for farmers like us who don't have to go looking for workers every year." Jake stopped, looking at Henry for approval.

"Seems like a mighty good plan, Jake. Walk with me a bit, there's something I'd like to ask you about the regular workers from around here." They began walking and Henry turned to Jake.

"Tell me, Jake, have you heard any rumblings about workers going someplace else to work next year? I have been hearing that there may be a crab house opening next summer. If this happens, do you think we'll lose many?"

"I've heard it's being built, but none of our workers have said anything. If they've heard, ain't nothing being said. There is a strange silence, but they do talk a lot in the fields, especially when they stop to eat. I thought it was because we brought in them new workers. But Mr. Pearson, if they can make more money, it's gonna be hard to hold them, even though some been with your family for a long time. Times been hard and what little they make in the summer gotta last all winter. I'll keep my ears open. Sure would be a sad day for farmers if that place opens." Jake stopped, not knowing what else to say or what Henry wanted to hear.

"Thanks, Jake. I'll be going now. Got to make many stops today."

"Bye, Mister Pearson." Jake returned to loading the trucks and Henry drove to the cannery where most of the women worked.

He decided to walk slowly through the plant and speak to the women. He hoped to pick up some feelings or attitudes. He really didn't know exactly what he was looking for, but he had to do something to help him make his decision.

He began walking through the wet aisles where the women were standing in their red-stained aprons with white caps covering their hair. "Good morning, ladies," he said cheerfully.

He stopped, "How are you ladies?" Some stopped and turned to face him, their hands filled with half-skinned steamed tomatoes.

"Fine I guess, Mister Henry," said one woman. "Don't see you 'round here much." Her dark face shone with perspiration from the summer heat and the steam. "My feet gets tired standing here all day. If we could sit down and work we sure would feel much more like working."

Henry did not reply, but moved on to the others. They all greeted him politely but in a cold, indifferent manner. Their lives were hard and the living such as it was came in seasons, like the crops.

He kept smiling as he entered the small office of the manager. As he entered, Jason jumped up to greet him.

"This is sure a real surprise, Mr. Pearson. Have a seat," Jason said anxiously as he pulled up a wooden, straight-backed chair. Henry sat down.

"Jason, how are things going here; are the women producing? They seemed a little hostile, even angry. Anything different happening here? Are you losing workers? Are you having a problem getting workers?" Henry stopped and waited for Jason to speak. Jason looked shocked at so many questions, questions that Henry had never asked before.

"Things don't change that much around here. We lose a few each year, but we always get new ones. They come here knowing it's seasonal work and it's better than working in the fields. Sure they act mad, and at times they get downright bad; but don't you worry, Mister Henry, I know how to handle these niggers. They gotta work. They want more money and shorter hours, but I just let 'em know they can go anytime—but they don't. They're lucky they got a job at all, and I let them know it every day. You ain't got nothing to worry about." Jason stopped talking, waiting for Henry to respond.

"Thanks, Jason. Tell me, have you heard them talk about the new crab house to be built in Merryneck? It could cause us some serious labor problems."

"These people around here don't know anything about crabs, Mister Henry. Most are afraid of them. They'd have to be trained, and that'd sure take a lot of time and money. I don't know how a company just getting started could do that. We might lose some if it happens, but not enough to hurt us. Besides, Merryneck is quite a distance. How they gonna get there? They can't walk so easy, and they don't have cars."

"Thanks, Jason, I must be going now, but I'll be seeing you again soon. Take care of yourself. I don't want to lose you." Henry shook hands with Jason and left.

Driving home he began to assess all he had seen and heard, but he still had no solution to the alarming situation. The route home took him past all the Pearson possessions, which were vast. His awareness of them was heightened as he thought of how much he had to lose and wondered how he was going to keep it. It was worth a fight, all he could give. But the question remained the same. How?

He had missed lunch, but food was not a part of his thoughts. His worries replaced his desire for food. An appetite for survival gripped his insides.

He arrived home in time for dinner, but he first had a strong drink and relaxed before attempting to eat. Alexander heard him and came to announce dinner.

"You dinner is ready, Mister Henry. You must be hungry 'cause you didn't come home for lunch. I sure hope everything is right with you. Will you be eatin' now or waitin'?"

"I'll be there in a moment. Just put the food on the table. I want to finish my drink. It's been a hard day, Alexander."

Mary brought the food and served it silently. "Mary, what did my uncle say about Ada?" Henry asked, observing the solemn look on her face.

"He said her heart is weak, her pressure is high and she should rest. No work for several weeks at least," she answered, not seeming to be aware of him, just talking as if to the wind. She was deeply engrossed in her thoughts and concern for her grandmother's condition, whom she loved more than her own mother.

"Will you be able to stay and help until she can return? It might interfere with your registering for college on time. You should write your mother and tell her what has happened first, then write the school and find out the last date for registration before you make any final decisions." Henry spoke calmly, trying not to upset her more and ease her fears.

"I'll write my mother, but I don't want to worry her unnecessarily until we find out how Grandma's coming along, or how serious it is. But I will write the school. Thank you for thinking of that. I have been so upset since we left Dr. Pearson's. He seemed so serious when he talked to us about her condition. No matter what happens, I'll not leave her until I am sure she'll be all right." Mary left the room hurriedly so he would not see her cry.

Henry followed her into the kitchen and sensed the strain she and Alexander were both under. He felt a need to make things a little easier for them somehow.

"Alexander, if Ada can't work and needs rest, who will look after her if both of you are here?"

"Aunt Ruth said she'd take care of her 'til she gets better. I jest hope you'll be satisfied with Mary helping me since I ain't so good at cooking. If you feels like you want to get somebody else to take her place..."

Henry interrupted him, "Don't worry about that, Alexander. I am sure Mary and you will do just fine. My needs are not that great at this time. From now until the end of the season I'll be away from home a great deal. There are some serious problems that I have to work out. I am sure we'll make out just fine. You just take care of Ada."

"Thank you, Mister Henry. I sure appreciates that and we'll keep things going for you," he replied gratefully.

Henry left the kitchen and returned to his dinner. He ate very little but he drank the coffee and ate a piece of apple pie. He just wanted another drink.

Mary returned to clear the table. She moved quickly and silently until Henry spoke to her.

"Mary, will you ask Alexander to come in."

"Yes, Mister Henry." She moved out quickly, as if the request was urgent.

"Mister Henry, Mary said you wanted to see me," said Alexander as he approached the chair where Henry sat slowly sipping his bourbon, blowing cigarette smoke, and looking pensively into space.

"Alexander, I hear they are building a crab house in Merryneck on the old Cummings plantation, that section located on the water where the oyster house is. I want you to drive down there with me tomorrow so I can see for myself what's going on."

"I'll gladly go, Mister Henry. I'd like to see myself. I been hearing some things, but nothin' for sure. What time you plan on leaving?"

60

"After breakfast will be time enough. I am going up now. You lock up before you and Mary leave."

"Good night, Mister Henry. Hope you gets a good night's sleep."

Henry poured another drink and took it upstairs with him, something he didn't usually do. But, he thought, I have never faced a situation like this before. If his father were living he would know what to do. His time and life had prepared him to handle such situations. Henry had to admit to himself in all honesty that he was totally confused, uncertain, and very frightened.

His room was filled with the bright glow of a summer moon. He undressed in its light and prepared for bed. But afterwards he sat in his chair and absorbed the crystal clear moonlight, hoping it would clear his head and thoughts with its brightness.

He reflected on his sudden decision to visit the Cummings place. He had not planned it or even thought of it until that moment he spoke to Alexander. How could he have made such an impetuous decision. But he had to know as much as possible about what was going on. He had to go; there was no other way.

There were times in the past when the Cummings family and his had been good friends. The two families had gone through the restoration period after the Civil War and survived. Frank Cummings had inherited his land and power from his father, the same as Henry had. He had had many good, productive years with the land until world War I. He had lost both of his sons and many of his Negro workers to the war. Many of the latter simply didn't come back. They went to Northern and Western cities seeking better jobs.

Cummings continued farming his land with the help he had left and new blacks migrating up from the deep South. They came with nothing and had no place to live when they got there, so he built shanty-type homes for them on the Rappahanock River that stretched along the front of his plantation. He built his own small community and became isolated with it. His land took on the appearance of a pre-Civil War plantation, his workers living and working there, except that they were paid and had the freedom to move about or leave if they wished.

Upkeep expenses forced Cummings to sell off much of his five thousand acres, but he had many acres left and at one time had been the Pearson Cannery's biggest supplier of string beans.

Cummings' isolation from the land gentry caused a lot of questions and suspicion among the other farmers. He was known as a bitter, lonely, but progressive man in his thinking about business and the management of workers. He built an oyster house, the only one in the county. It provided employment in the winter for the Negroes who worked the farm in the summer. This arrangement helped to insure that his workers would not leave. He taught his Negro workers how to net oysters and shuck them, and some were trained in sales work, selling oysters throughout the county and the state.

Each year Cummings sold more land to buy boats, trucks, and other equipment to improve production and delivery of the oysters and his harvest. His community remained separate, but unthreatening—until now. Many big farmers resented him for his move from land to the rivers that supplied even more in production than farming.

It was well known that Cummings had taught Negro men to fish for a living, and that these men were now leaving him for full summer work with the big fishing companies in other parts of the state. They could live on the fishing boats the whole summer, saving all their earnings. He had felt this loss during the planting and harvesting season since the men did not return home until September. Henry thought, he'll bring them back and even attract more workers with a full summer of crabbing, picking, packing and hauling and full-time work in the oyster house in the winter. "He is smart as hell," Henry said aloud. It was obvious to him that Cummings was moving with the times and its needs rather than holding onto a past that was facing painful and obvious decay."

Evidently Cummings' cousin had great vision and influence in this new industry. He must have the financial resources necessary for such a bold venture.

Henry wondered if he should diversify and to what? He wanted desperately to talk with Cummings; he might learn something that could help resolve his painful dilemma.

That night sleep cruelly evaded Henry again, leaving him with tortured thoughts of his plight and his inherited responsibilities. He felt painfully inadequate to handle the sudden changes that threatened his existence. He had never been trained to handle change, only to maintain the status quo. His inherited legacy had outlived its time and now became a burning burden to perpetuate a dying system that built a past, without plans for a future.

Chapter Six

Henry's visit with Cummings made him realize even more the depth of his situation and its many frightening ramifications. He understood and appreciated Cummings decision to develop another industry, but it left him even more confused about his fate.

Before he could make a final decision or plans for future industrialization the landowners began their plan of action. Word spread like wildfire, and anger and fear followed in its wake. The major landowners evicted those they thought might consider working at the crab house. The community was consumed by fear and uncertainty, and Henry knew the council of farmers would be watching him to see if he was adhering to their plan.

Each member of the council evicted one family from the land they had occupied for several generations. Negro families selected for the power play were those who were renting and had the largest families. In some cases the families were given six months to pay off their debt, if they wanted to buy the land they lived on. Knowing that they couldn't pay in that span of time with the kind of money they earned, the council felt secure and smug.

The word of this action resounded throughout the county. Everyone was baffled as to the reason behind it, creating a hostile and angry climate that was set to explode like an untimed bomb.

The harvest season was over and the workers scattered. Their plans weren't known to the council, and the secrecy was more than they could bear. A council meeting was called again at the Lawsons for the purposes of having Henry declare his intentions and solidifying their efforts against the Negroes. As Henry entered the room, he was not surprised by the atmosphere of extreme hostility he felt directed toward him.

They greeted each other—then all eyes and attention were directed toward him.

"You betrayed us. You did nothing that we agreed to do," Lawson yelled at Henry, his face turning red and the veins standing out on his neck. "You, of all people, can't lose workers. You have the most to lose if your workers go to the crab house. I don't understand your actions and what you have done to our plans."

"Henry, you and I own most of the land in this section of the county, and we have the greatest control over land sales," Boyd Pearson added angrily. "Many rent from us; the Negroes are buying or just living on our land. Your father, my brother, would stop at nothing to keep his power and control. You don't act like a true Pearson."

"Henry, just what do you plan to do about this disastrous situation?" asked Senator Morris.

"I really don't know, but I know this way is not the answer. I just know some changes must be made.

Uncle Boyd pays his help four dollars a week—for six days. Some of us pay ten cents an hour. It takes ten hours to make a dollar. And the tomato pickers get less. This is another form of slavery and time demands some change. The only way you have been able to keep these workers is by Cummings giving them winter work in the oyster house. We can't stop the crab house, and what you all are doing won't stop them. We have got to make changes. Time won't hold back just for us. I must find my own way to solve this problem. I have got to salvage my farm, the grain mill and the cannery. I need more workers than any of you, but putting the people off the land, leaving them with no place to go, is not the answer for me or for them. We are not sure they'll be leaving, but your tactics are forcing them to do just that."

"Henry, you are either with us or you are not, that's your decision. We'll just count you out. I mean out of everything. You can consider our friendship over," said Lawson, who had assumed the leadership role for the group.

"Gentlemen, I am sorry you feel that way toward me. I don't want to lose your friendship, but I must find solutions to my problems in my own way. Good night," Henry said and left the house.

On his way home, Henry felt grateful for the night—the darkness was like a cloak shielding and protecting him from the attacks he would face.

His decision not to join the others had not occurred to him until he had met with them. There was a sudden force in him that had taken over and the words had just come out effortlessly. Now he would have to fight the battle alone. There was no comfort in the decision he had made.

He thought of his Uncle Boyd, who along with Henry's father had struggled to regain their land, their homes, their power, and the extension of that power by acquiring most of the land in that section of the county by any means. Yet they had made it possible for many Negroes to buy land, and others who rented were never pressured for payments when times were hard. A bond of trust based on mutual need had been established between the Pearsons and their workers, and they had learned over the years to rely on each other. It had become an unspoken love-hate code on both sides.

It was hard for Henry to accept his uncle's role in this self-defeating plan. It was unbelievable that he felt so threatened that he would take such drastic measures. It was a great power play between a simple seafood company and the notable landed gentry, with the Negroes caught in the middle since neither business could exist without cheap labor.

The impending changes were destined to affect the economic status of the county. The summer was productive, but now the land lay bare as if raped and abused. It evidenced such painful neglect that he almost cried.

Henry didn't look forward to the winter of discontent, anger and uncertainty that loomed ahead. It would have to be his quiet time for evaluating and making painful decisions for survival. He began to think of Martha, about his relationship with her and her father's bitter feelings toward him. He felt empty and lonely already; it was a silent prelude to what was to come.

Henry thought today would be a good one to spend with Martha. As he drove he became a little apprehensive about Martha's attitude toward him since his riff with her father. His need for her was growing stronger, as if willed by the approaching season of conflict.

Martha greeted him coldly and he felt a shiver invade his warm emotions, but his need urged him on.

"Henry, you have a nerve coming here after what you have done. Father told me how you betrayed them." She trembled with conflicting emotions of anger and love.

"I never betrayed them. I just didn't agree with their plans. Futile and vindictive plans that are neither good business nor humane. What does it have to do with us?" he asked, looking directly into her eyes.

"It has everything to do with us. My father does not want me to see you anymore. It's evident that you have a different set of values than the rest of us. You have made it impossible for us to continue our relationship. Father will not hear of it and all your friends here feel the same way. Henry, you have lost all your friends."

"I am not so concerned about them as I am about us. True, I do not agree with the others in this matter, but in time things will mend. No matter how we feel, changes come. Sure they threaten us—I have as much to lose as the rest—but you must see that we have to change our way of life if we are to survive or advance." He moved closer to Martha and reached out to touch her, but she pulled away.

"I am part of this way of life, a system that we both have lived in for generations. I do love you, Henry; I have for most of my adult life and even longer, but I am a product of this system and will defend it at any cost." She turned, avoiding his searching eyes.

"You mean that your love is determined by our economic system?" he asked, probing for deeper meanings.

"We *are* the system; we developed it and we must protect it. You can't just surrender a way of life without a fight."

"Even though it's a fight you can't win? I plan to fight, but in a different way. Who is to decide what is the right way?"

"Everyone seems to think you have some secret plan that you won't tell them; since you are not joining them, you must be planning against them." Anger sparked her words.

"I am not against them. I just don't agree with their methods. Can't you understand that? The Civil War split our country over the issue of slave labor. Now this county is split by the agricultural and seafood industries, but the issue is still the same: our dependency on black labor. That's our way of life, and that's what needs to change."

"Don't say any more, just leave. You'll regret your stand. You'll not survive by yourself."

Henry left the house without another word. It was useless to continue.

She was right, though, Henry thought as he drove home. They had made the system, and if the system died, they would die. But the hope he felt lie in the possibility of creating a new system, one that could move forward into the future.

Henry could see the signs that a new system was emerging, one that might free both the whites and the Negroes from their unwilling dependence. The newly emerging industry may not be the answer for blacks, but it offered them a choice; and that was a big step toward their economic growth and independence.

Morning came, bringing welcome relief from a night filled with disturbing thoughts and unresolved problems. Henry was happy to see Mary and Alexander, although they were preoccupied with their concern over Ada's lack of progress. Mary had assumed almost absolute control of managing the house and did so with astonishing efficiency. Alexander was showing signs of severe depression over

Ada's failing condition and his work had slowed down.

Henry entered the kitchen unnoticed; Mary was busy preparing his breakfast and Alexander was checking his outside chores.

"Good morning, Mary," he said casually.

She turned, startled. "Good morning, Mister Henry. I didn't hear you come in. Your breakfast is ready. Have a seat and I'll bring it in."

"No, Mary. I'll eat in here today. I want to talk to you about your plans for school."

"Mister Henry, I really don't know what to do. Grandma is not getting better and I can't leave her. I'll just have to start next semester. Grandpa can't take care of her alone. I have written to my mother and told her about my plans. She understands."

"I am so sorry, Mary. You have done a fine job here, but I suppose you have no other choice. I am sure things will work out for the best. Uncle Boyd is keeping a close watch on Ada. I know he'll do all he can for her."

"Good morning, Mister Henry," said Alexander in a surprised tone. "I didn't expect to see you eating in the kitchen."

"I wanted a chance to talk to you and Mary about Ada."

"She seems mighty low to me. She don't seem to be getting well at all. She's got me worried. Dr. Boyd says her heart is weak and it may take a long time for her to get better. I jest keep praying. She is so worn out; life has been hard for us."

"I know it's been hard for both of you, but you have done much better than many others. Try not to worry too much. Uncle Boyd will keep an eye on her."

"I guess we is both jest tired and worn out. I ain't been feeling so good myself lately, but we jest gotta keep on till the good Lord says it's our time."

"Tell me, Alexander, what have you heard about

70

the new crab house? Do you think many of your people will go there to work?"

"Most in Bungle Hook won't be going. Many are too old, and some still work their own land. There are only a couple of people who might go . . . unless more are forced to," Alexander spoke in a restrained tone, not wanting to say too much.

"Have you heard of anyone being forced off their land or losing their homes?" Henry asked anxiously, trying to find out what affect the council's edict was having on the community and how feelings were running toward the big farmers.

"It's being said around that some folks are gonna lose their homes if they can't pay up their payments. But jest about all of us in Bungle Hook own our land and homes free and clear. We was able to get land right after the war, but most others couldn't buy. It's so terrible for this to happen when folks were jest getting on their feet after the depression. It's such a mean, sinful thing to do to poor folks."

"Alexander, what will they do if they lose their homes?"

"We've always found a way; this ain't the first time somethin' like this done happened to us. Well, I guess I'd better go back and finish my work, Mister Henry." He left quickly to escape a discussion that caused him mixed feelings.

Henry turned to Mary, "What do you think of all this?"

"It just seems like slavery will never end. People are always having their lives uprooted," she said angrily. "Seems that's an uncalled-for thing to do. I don't know too much about it, but it seems a sure way to keep the hate going." She stopped talking and began clearing the table.

Henry realized he would get no more from either of them. He had needed to know what direction the fatal plan was taking and the reaction of the Negroes about the critical situation. He had thought Alexander might be a good source.

Henry went to his study to work on plans for the next season and check his business accounts, but his thoughts did not take that direction. He returned instead to the morning's conversations: to Mary and the unexpected hostility that was so out of character for her, and Alexander's uneasiness. He couldn't feel any real disappointment in their response since no one ever really knew how the Negro felt about the system that had kept the races separate for hundreds of years. Though the Negroes and the whites had one of the closest personal relationships in history, they were never emotionally or socially close. For many years the Negro's private thoughts and feelings were the only things he could call his own, and he protected them with guarded silence. Actually, both Alexander and Mary had been extremely open with him, Henry thought, considering the sensitive nature of the topic.

Negroes had nursed, raised and nurtured white families for generations, yet they were worlds apart. Even though whole families had been entrusted to their care, they were still not treated or considered really human. Why should Mary and Alexander tell him anything that would help him—he was still considered the enemy.

He had always needed the Negro workers for his cannery, but the thought crossed his mind that he might be able to work with Negro farmers as well. It would be cheaper for him to buy tomatoes from them than to grow the crop himself and hire pickers, especially if workers were scare next year due to the crab house.

The Negroes who owned their land would not be run off by the council, Henry knew. They had the same pride in land ownership as the landed gentry and would fight just as hard to keep it.

The poor whites were just the opposite: they refused to struggle to improve their status because they thought such a struggle would put them in the same category with the Negro. They preferred to oversee the Negro workers, not to do the same work. Because of that, Henry knew they would not seek jobs in the new seafood industry or work the farms. Some would rather die—and many had—rather than be field workers.

The survival of both the large landowners and the seafood industry depended on Negro labor. His task would be to convince the few Negro landowners to grow crops that needed to be picked, or even to become tenant farmers on his land for those crops.

Then his mind wandered to thoughts of Mary: her spunk, her deep love for her family, her quiet pride and dignity. She was unusual, different from any woman he had ever known, and he had known many. Her exquisite beauty was quiet and refined, but also disturbing and exciting. He saw in her defiance and strength, as well as courage.

The atmosphere of the house had changed since Mary had come. Her presence gave him a sense of security for some reason. He wanted her to stay. He had found himself becoming more aware of her influence on his life and mentally struggled to analyze it. Was it the comfortable pleasure of having a good servant, or was it something else? The last thought he rejected with almost violent haste. Without reason, he stormed angrily out of the house.

His unscheduled drive took him to his grain mill. It was the one business he felt secure about, since there was no other grain mill for many miles. All the farmers, large and small, black and white, depended on it for milling their wheat and corn. And if the pickers went to work in the seafood houses, grain would become the dominate crop since it could be harvested with machinery.

"Madison, what do you think about expanding the mill? I have a feeling there'll be a real need for it soon." Madison had been the manager of the mill since his father first started it and Henry valued his opinion.

"Business has been increasing lately, but expansion would mean we'd have to buy more equipment and hire more workers. But we could probably attract white workers if the Negroes still did the heavy work."

"Do you think we'll lose the Negroes when the crab house opens?"

"No, these men are strong and they like to show their strength. They figures nobody else can do it but them. That crab house work's not for them; besides, the better jobs there will be given to white men. Anyhow, the Negroes know they got no other place to get their meal and flour but here. If I was you, I'd show them you have the power to refuse to mill their grain—like the others are doing about their rent and payments—just in case any of them are thinking of leaving. Ain't no place these Negroes can turn to except people like you if they want to live. You'll get as many workers as you need if you want to expand."

"We do have the power of life and death over them. It must be pretty frightening."

"For damn sure. Got that right, Mister Henry. Cut 'em off, that's what your father would have done. He knew how to handle them. He kept them in line." Madison smirked arrogantly.

Henry suddenly saw Madison through new eyes and didn't like the picture. He felt himself growing hot with anger.

"No intimidation, Madison." he said firmly. "If I

74

find out that you're threatening any of our workers you'll be fired immediately. Now, we'll begin making plans for the expansion of the mill in time for next summer's crops. Outline your needs and expenses and have them ready for me next week."

Madison was surprised at the sudden change in Henry. He was used to manipulating the young heir. Madison's tone was surly as he nodded his head and said simply, "Yes, Mister Henry."

"Fine, I'll see you next week."

Returning to the house in almost desperate flight, Henry immediately called Alexander to his den.

"You want me, Mister Henry? I thought you'd gone out. I had no idea you was home. Is there something you want? You sounded like it was powerful important."

"Come in; I want to talk to you. You know lots of people like yourself, Negroes who own their own land. I have an idea. I plan to ask the Negro farmers to grow tomatoes and sell them to me for my cannery. I feel the number of pickers I need for my own fields are going to be hard to get."

"They would do it, Mister Henry, if they could be sure you'd buy the whole crop. My two sons is tending my land these days. They'd be mighty happy to grow tomatoes if they knew for sure you'd buy 'em. Sure costs a lot to raise a big crop like you's gonna need."

"I know this is something new, Alexander, but I need all the tomato crops I can get next summer. I'll assure them that their investments would pay off. I plan to meet and talk to them. I'll explain everything, don't worry. I can see some real changes taking place around here."

"I ain't sure, Mister Henry. Suppose it's a bad season and they lose everything? It's sure a big chance. They gonna need money to get started, and where's that coming from. I jest don't know."

"I can't guarantee the weather, but farming always has that risk. I can lend them money to get started; that's the chance I'm willing to take. But I also think this is an opportunity for your people to get more independent. You get your sons together and I'll talk to them."

"Yes, Mister Henry. I'll tell them. I am only sorry I can't work my own land any more. That land means a lot to me and my family. We've all worked hard for it. It sure would be good if it could really make more money, 'specially since Ada's ailing so badly."

"Well, you let me know when and where to meet them. I am sure we can work something out. Thanks, Alexander, you've been helpful."

Alexander left the room feeling suspended somewhere between hope and fear. It seemed he had always lived in the limbo world between hope and despair.

When the phone rang, Henry jumped. He was irritated by the rude intrusion on his thoughts. "Yes," he said curtly. "Mr. Lawson. This is a surprise. Haven't heard from you for quite a while. How are you?"

Lawson asked him to come to an emergency council meeting the next night at his house.

"Are you sure you want me to come? I am surprised after our last meeting. Yes, I'll be there." He hung up, wondering what was going on and why he was asked. But he would go. He was anxious to hear how their plan was working and needed to find out the tone of events in order to plan his moves—and he also felt the need of contact with his friends.

Dinner was pensive, almost solemn. Mary was distantly polite, her lovely smile withheld. Henry restricted his requests in respect for her concern about Ada. Her devotion to her grandmother was deep. He admired her for that—and envied Ada. He had never felt such devotion for anyone, but he had longed for it.

The dark veil of night draped the house, and Henry surrendered to it completely, relinquishing all concerns and stresses of recent weeks.

The morning sun caressed him with a warm and gentle touch, urging him out of bed. For the first time in weeks Henry felt hopeful about resolving his problems, and he willingly responded to the beckoning day. It was comforting to know he was still included in the circle, and he was anxious to see his friends.

However, Henry's smile was short-lived. The group of landowners in the living room of the Lawson home looked grim and angry, as if readying for an attack. He greeted all of them and then sat down, reluctant to ask what the problem was.

Lawson spoke as if addressing a political assembly, "Gentlemen, we've suffered a serious blow to our plans, and I sure hope you have some solutions." He picked up two newspapers and held them up. "There are two newspapers published in Richmond. One is Negro, the other a major and respected newspaper in this state. Each has an article on what we are doing to prevent the Negroes from leaving the land. We are painted as old slave masters in both papers. I want to know how they got this information." He looked around room, directly at each person, silently demanding an answer.

Senator Morris was the first to respond, "There's nothing illegal about what we are doing, and there's nothing anyone can do about it. I don't like it, but we have nothing to fear from a few city liberals. I should be the most concerned, since I am a member of the state legislature. In fact, the information was probably supplied by one of my political opponents in an attempt to discredit me."

"I still don't like it," Lawson yelled. "I want to know what we can do to stop this."

"Have your plans been effective?" Henry asked curiously. "Are you getting the results you wanted?"

"I don't know for sure; you never know what those damned coloreds are thinking. But I do know it's nobody's business what we do in this county. If our Negroes get hold of articles like this, they'll get ideas and be harder to control than ever."

"I don't like it either," Boyd Pearson said calmly. "But to tell the truth, I don't know what we can do about it. At this point the papers have no facts; nothing has happened to provoke an investigation. They are only dealing with hearsay."

"I am going to say it again: we have got to face the fact that change is descending on us without regard for our personal wishes," Henry said. He had planned not to get involved in the discussion, but their unbending attitude drove him to try to make them understand. "We must change in order to survive. All of you are aware, even more than I am, of the history of our state on the question of slavery and the attitudes that have existed since reconstruction. We strongly opposed emancipation and then used the Negroes as political tools when they got the right to vote in spite of us, that is until the poll tax effectively took that away from them.

"From 1865 till now our state's laws have concentrated on destroying the Negroes, from disenfranchising them to the total destruction of all their civil and economic rights. We have tried extermination through starvation and lynching, and we were the last state to rejoin the union after the war. All this makes us, the landowners especially, a target from many liberals."

"What the hell does that have to do with what's happening now?" Lawson demanded, standing and waving his arms frantically.

"It's got every damn thing to do with it," Henry shot back. "If we lose the Negro labor, we lose our wealth, our property, our livelihood. Our positions are built on the backs of the Negroes. We have let ourselves become so dependent on them that we are terrified at the thought of losing their cheap labor; we've just become damned lazy and blind. We can't even think of others ways to keep what we have, such as growing crops that don't require cheap labor for harvesting. I know I am the youngest here, but I see change as inevitable. However, it doesn't have to mean our destruction, and that's what we should be dealing with here." Henry stopped suddenly. Looking at there faces, he could see their resentment; it was useless to continue.

"You sound like a nigger-lover to me. No white man in your position talks that stuff," screamed Lawson, pointing an accusing finger at Henry as he stood in the middle of the floor. "Your father would be ashamed of you if he were here. It must be that nigger gal you got working at your house. People been talking about how you look at her and treat her. God knows what else has been going on there since her mammy's been sick."

"That's enough, John," Boyd Pearson said firmly. "There's no need for this, and I don't want to hear any more accusations. It's got nothing to do with our problem here, so shut up and sit down. You are acting like a crazy man. We've got to stick together if we are going to win this battle!" Pearson was angry but held it in control. He was in this too deep and had no intention of alienating his life-long friends, even for his nephew.

"Good night," Henry said stiffly, his hands clenched by his sides. "Let me know when you want to talk reasonably about our business problem. That's what this is, or what it should be—not an issue of race or hatred or sex. In case you've forgotten, many of these Negroes are your descendants or your fathers' descendants. Sex with a Negro woman is nothing new to any of you. I strongly resent your accusation about my relationship with Mary, Mr. Lawson, but you can be assured that if it were true, I would never hide it behind hypocrisy as some others have done." With that Henry left the house, burning with resentment and anger. He felt disappointed—he had been so hopeful that their differences would be resolved.

As he lay awake once again, his night thoughts centered on the fear that was keeping the council members from thinking logically. He saw it turning to hate and anger, and he knew that, unless it were stopped, it would erupt in violence with neither side emerging victorious.

His thoughts turned to Mary. It was his responsibility to protect her. If the rumors grew, it could be disastrous for her. He felt no fear for himself, but he knew that Mary should leave here. He would not allow her to be degraded as so many others had been. If only he didn't feel so empty at the thought of her absence.

Chapter Seven

The early morning silence was shattered by Mary hysterically calling Henry's name as she ran through the Pearson mansion. Startled out of sleep, he jumped out of bed and rushed downstairs. Mary was standing at the bottom of the long, winding staircase in a state of extreme agitation.

"Please, Mister Henry, get your uncle to come right away. I think Grandma is dying. Please hurry, Mr. Henry. I don't think we have much time."

"All right, Mary. I'll call him. Stay here and calm down, please." Mary followed him into the study while he called Dr. Pearson. He concluded the call and turned to her.

"Mary, Uncle Boyd said he will go to the house immediately. Maybe it's not as bad as you think. He'll do the best he can. I am so sorry; I had no idea she had taken a turn for the worst. Mary, I'll do everything I can to help you."

"Mister Henry, I do appreciate your help, but I

don't think she's going to make it this time, and she wants you to come to the house. She wants to talk with you, and she says it's important. You must come. I have got to get back now." She turned and quickly left the house, driving her grandparents' old Model T.

Henry felt the urgency of the situation and dressed quickly for the ride to a place about which he knew little. He had often heard his father talk about Bungle Hook, whose residents had all purchased their land from the Pearsons. The free-born Negroes there had pretty much cut themselves off from the mainstream of Forrestville.

The road from the highway was narrow, really developed only for wagons. He drove for about a mile until he reached a section of homesteads that had been carved out of the wilderness. The fields looked productive; the lawns were green; and colorful flower gardens decorated many front yards. It was picturesque, quiet and peaceful—and safe from outside intrusion.

Henry recognized Alexander's car in the yard and drove the short lane to a small, two-story, English-style house with white shingles. As he drove to the side of the house to park, he saw that a second screened porch connected the main house to the kitchen, a common design in that area. They were watching and waiting for him, and Mary came out to greet him.

"Please come this way, Mister Henry. Your uncle hasn't come yet, but Grandma wants to see you," Mary said as Henry followed her through the dining room and up the stairs to Ada's room.

She was lying in a bed with a high headboard made of dark, highly polished mahogany. A thick feather mattress covered with a brightly colored, handmade bedspread dominated the scene. Ada's long gray hair was braided; it highlighted her beautiful olive skin and Henry could see the racial mixture in her facial structure more clearly than ever.

Mary pulled up a chair for him close enough to the bed so he could hear Ada's weak and fading voice.

"It was so good of you to come, Mister Henry. I know I have little time left. I just want you to make sure Mary gets in school She's lost so much time for me, but you can help her when I'm gone. She'll be the first of the family to go to college. She can't miss this chance. She is a precious child; I want a better life for her. This is no place for her. I want you to make sure she gets that chance." She stopped talking. Her breath came in short gasps and her weak, gray-blue eyes looked at him pleadingly.

"Don't worry, Ada, I understand. I'll make sure she gets her chance. Don't talk any more. Uncle Boyd should be here soon. He'll take good care of you. You'll get better," he said unconvincingly. But his real feelings were far from the words he spoke. The restrictions of his culture did not allow him to express how deeply he would miss her when she was gone. She was a Negro. They both understood.

"There is money in the bank in her name. Don't let nothing happen to it; we've all worked so hard for it—her mother and Alexander and me. Mister Henry, I trust you to do this for me. She's got to have a better life."

Dr. Pearson entered the room. "I'll wait for you downstairs, Uncle Boyd," Henry said.

Walking through the house alone, Henry observed how well kept it was and how tastefully furnished. He walked out to the porch where Mary and Alexander were sitting in solemn silence.

"I'll wait here for Uncle Boyd," he said awkwardly.

"Have a seat, Mister Henry. It's cooler here than in the house. I'll get you a cold glass of lemonade."

He accepted it, but could not feel comfortable in this situation. This was a new experience for him. All his previous relationships with Negroes were as worker and employer. The gap between them was hard to bridge even in this simple social situation. They were conditioned to keep their polite distance and so was he. So they all sat in silence until his uncle came down.

"Alexander," Dr. Pearson said in a deeply sympathetic voice, "I have done all I can. She won't last long, I'm afraid. Her heart is very weak—she is just worn out. Try to make her as comfortable as possible; that's about all you can do now."

He walked to the door of the porch and stood for a moment looking at the field. "You sure have done a great job with the land. I never thought anything could be done with it when I sold it to you, Alexander. It was nothing but woods. It sure must have taken a lot of hard work to turn it into a successful farm."

"Thank you, Dr. Pearson. This land's been our life, and it's paid off. I jest don't know what I am gonna do if Ada dies. But at least my sons and their children tend the it now."

"Coming, Henry?"

"Yes, Uncle Boyd." They both left. Henry was relieved to depart the uncomfortable situation, but he wished there were some way he could express his real feelings for those wonderful people.

"Mary, you look after your grandmother. I'll do the chores before lunch."

"Yes, Grandpa." Mary knew this was his way of handling grief. For Alexander, work was a cure-all, especially where emotions were concerned.

Mary went upstairs to her grandmother's room and sat beside the bed watching her sleep. She picked up Ada's tanned and wrinkled hand and stroked it with loving gentleness. She remembered her younger years and summers spent amidst the love in this house. She could never imagine life without this gentle but strong woman who had filled her life with love and security. She began to cry quietly, loneliness now filling her with impeccable sadness.

Ada stirred, slowly opening her eyes. "Don't cry, Baby. Grandma is ready to go. I just hate to leave you. You've been such a joy in my life. You are so sweet and loving. Baby, Grandma's ready. I am going home to my God and be free at last."

"Oh, Grandma, please don't leave me. Life would be so empty. You made it so worthwhile." She took her grandmother in her arms like a child, rocking her back and forth in the prologue to death. She felt Ada cough three times, and then she went limp. Silence followed, the silence that heralds the spirit's passing when the body is claimed by death.

Mary still held the lifeless body, refusing to relinquish it to unknown eternity. She gently laid her back on the bed, stroked her hair, kissed her, and sat silently—not wanting to share this time with anyone.

The sun was bright and its warm, comforting glow penetrated the silence. "'Tis done," Mary said to herself, now ready for the tasks that lay ahead. Somehow she felt her grandmother would always be with her, and maybe somewhere they would meet again. Such bonds could not be broken, even by death.

Mary walked slowly and quietly down the steps, not wanting to disturb the silence. She consoled herself with the thought that her grandmother's memory was not just of the present moment, but would be a part of so many memories yet unborn.

She went to the back yard where her grandfather was hoeing the garden. He was such a hard worker, and he loved the land and took pride in his ownership.

She stopped and watched him for a moment. The sun glistened on his mixed gray hair, his sun-tanned skin. He was a handsome man whose back had begun to bend from many hard years of trying to make things grow in a hostile and infertile land.

Touching him gently on the shoulder, Mary said calmly, "Grandpa. Grandma is gone."

"Oh! Dear God, dear God, chile." He dropped the hoe and his gray-blue eyes filled with tears.

Sorrow enveloped them as they walked silently back to the house. They sat at the porch table. Mary got up to get him a cold glass of lemonade. As he drank, she stroked his head.

"Chile, what we gonna do without her?'

"I'll be with you. I won't leave you. We'll make out."

Alexander finished his drink, got up and went into the house to spend his last moments with the woman who had shared his life for more than fifty years.

Mary realized the things that had to be done: she must call her mother and tell her uncles, but first she would tell Aunt Ruth and the relatives and neighbors in their small community.

Once again Mary walked the path through the wheat field to Aunt Ruth's house. She called out as she entered through the back porch, trying not to startle her.

"Aunt Ruth, Grandma has passed. Will you stay with Grandpa while I go to tell the family?"

"Oh, chile, I just had a feeling. She'd been so sick, but God knows best. We been back here in these woods together for many years. I don't know how I'd have made out if it hadn't been for her. She was a wonderful woman, but she sure earned this rest. Oh Lord, I'll miss her. I'll jest be lost, but I suppose my time won't be long coming. You've been her pride and joy since you was born. She always spoke of you so highly. 'Such a pretty girl, such a sweet chile,' she would say. You brought so much joy to her life."

"We'd better go, Aunt Ruth. I have so much to do," Mary said, starting for the door.

While they were walking back to the house, Ruth reminded Mary to call the undertaker. "You'll have to drive over, it's so far. You been there before. He's the only Negro undertaker in these parts. Mary, stop and get your cousin Gladys. She's been carrying the mail in these parts and knows her way around. Besides, I don't really think you'll be able to concentrate on your driving right now."

Mary left Ruth at the house and drove to the Pearson estate. Henry was sitting in the breakfast room reading and was startled to see her.

"Mister Henry, Grandma has passed. I need to call my mother in Baltimore. May I use your phone, please."

"Sure, Mary, help yourself. I am truly sorry about your Grandmother. I'll miss her so much," he said sincerely.

Mary went to the study and called her mother. After a short but emotional conversation, she hung up and returned to the room where Henry was waiting.

"Mister Henry, how can I call the undertaker?"

"I know who he is. I'll get the call through for you."

When the connection was made, he gave Mary the phone. She made the necessary arrangements and quickly hung up.

"Thank you, Mister Henry, but I must run. There's so much to do."

"I understand, Mary. Let me know if you need me for anything. Don't worry about me. We'll talk when this is over." He wanted to hold and console her, but he dared not.

Mary drove directly to Cousin Gladys' house. Gladys had secured a government contract to deliver mail five years ago and she was the only woman with such a job, as well as the only Negro. She had enjoyed going on rounds with Gladys when she was a child. She had taken Mary's grandmother with her sometimes so she could shop. It was always an interesting outing, seeing the pretty homes of the whites, even meeting some who would come out and talk to Gladys. She shared news and gossip with them. They all seemed to like her and often gave her things they'd baked. Mary would eat ice cream and drink pop when they stopped at stores or filling stations, and the owners would never let Gladys pay them. Mary learned that only whites got their mail deliveried; Negroes had to walk to the post office housed in the main store.

Mary knocked on the back porch door and went in. Gladys came to the door sipping a beer.

"Mary, what brings you here this time of day? Come on in; it's been a long time since I have seen you. How's cousin Ada? I been meaning to get there, but after my mail route, I have to work in the house."

"Gladys, Grandma died this morning."

"Dear God, I sure loved Cousin Ada. She was always so good to me."

"I know; she was loved by many. I need your help. Will you take me to the minister's house—I don't know exactly where he lives—then to my uncle's? I'd rather not drive."

"Sure, Mary, but first we must call Cousin Ada's sisters and relatives in Northumberland."

"But they don't have phones."

"That's true, but one of your cousins there has a store. I am sure they have a phone. Let's try. You just set there and rest; I'll take care of it."

Mary was content to sit and look out at the

sprawling fields. Ernest, Gladys' husband, had acquired large quantities of land with the help of his three brothers. When the others moved to the city, Ernest managed the farm, and he had made it quite profitable.

"Mary, that's all taken care of. Your cousin Jane will tell the others. Now, let's go see Reverend Jordan."

They got in Gladys' car and drove to another section of the county called Molusk. When they reached the house, they were greeted by Mrs. Jordan.They hurriedly explained their mission, but she informed them that Reverend Jordon was at another funeral and wouldn't be back until late. She said she would give him the message. She expressed her sympathy and assured them he would come see them as soon as he returned.

"Thank you so much, Mrs. Jordan. I do appreciate your help. Goodbye."

They began their drive to Kilmonarch, the large town where James, her older uncle, lived. It was about twenty-five miles away. The drive was lovely, and as they drove, Gladys pointed out homes of the white people she knew.

Uncle James had wanted to remain on the land and had bought in Kilmonarch because he did not like living in Bungle Hook. His brother Spencer had left also and lived in Lively, ten miles away.

The Negroes in Kilmonarch seemed more progressive and had better jobs in the business section, but many were not land owners. It was a center for business where farmers could buy equipment and sell their produce.

James had a fifty-acre farm close to the schools and the market. His small bungalow was enough for him, his wife, and their son and daughter. His wife Shirley greeted them at the door and invited them onto the back porch. She was in the process of finishing her daily house chores before the children came home from school.

"Shirley, is James around?"

"Yes, Mary, he's just in the barn feeding the horses. I'll get him. Is something wrong? You look upset?"

"Grandma died this morning and I came to tell him."

"Oh, Mary, James will be so upset. He worshiped his mother. They all did. I'll get him."

She returned quickly with James rushing ahead of her.

"Mary, what happened? I thought she was getting better," he demanded with tears filling his brown eyes. He pushed back his curly brown hair in distraction. "I am going up there right now, Shirley. I'll be back sometime tonight. You tell the children."

"Aunt Ruth is with Grandpa, Uncle James, and I'll stop on my way back to tell Uncle Spencer. I have taken care of most things, with Gladys' help. I'll see you at the house."

After James left, Mary and Gladys said goodbye and drove to Spencer's 75-acre farm in Lively. He had wanted to leave Bungle Hook too, but he had also felt strongly protective of his parents and did not want to move too far away. Mary's mother, Rachel, had been the one who hated the farming life. She was the oldest and the only one to leave. All were profoundly bound to their parents, especially to their mother, Ada.

"Gladys, I can't thank you enough for driving me all over. I know you must get home for supper. I'll only be a minute at Uncle Spencer's."

"That's all right, Mary. I am glad I could help. Your grandmother was a good friend to me when I married Ernest. I was from another county and it was hard to get to know people. I think it was because I was much younger than he was and they didn't know anything about me. But Ada was kind and we became good friends, especially when she went with me on my mail routes. I could talk to her about my feelings and fears. She always had open and welcoming arms for me. If there's anything I can do for her family, I'll do it gladly."

"Thanks, Gladys. We are just about there. I do hope Uncle Spencer's home."

They drove into the yard and entered the screened porch from the front, since it went completely around the house. Mary called for Spencer's wife, Marion, but Spencer himself answered the hail. They all sat on the white porch furniture that Spencer had built. Furniture building was his second occupation and he sold quite a bit of it in the winter when he wasn't farming.

"Uncle Spencer, I came to let you know that Grandmother died this morning."

"What! Good God, Mary, it can't be!" His blue eyes glistened with tears. He dropped his head between his hands and sobbed like a little boy. His reddish blond hair sparkled in the bright sunlight, making his bent head glow like a ball of gold. He looked so much like her mother: their hair and eyes were the same color and they both had freckles.

"Uncle Spencer, I must leave now so Gladys can get back. Maybe you and Marion can come up later. There are some things we need to talk about."

"I'll be there as soon as Marion returns with the car. I'll get myself together by then. Thanks, Gladys. It's kind of you to help Mary."

"I'll see you later at the house," Mary said as they left him alone with his grief.

They passed the church on the way back, and Mary remembered there was a family plot in the graveyard. Grandpa had set it aside for him and Ada and other members of the family.

"Mary, you know Cousin Ada was a member of the House of Ruth. They should be notified since they have a special service for deceased members."

"Oh, I didn't know that, but I do remember being in the Tom Thumb weddings when I was little. I don't know who to contact, do you?"

"Yes. The lodge is near my house. I'll tell them; don't worry."

At Gladys' house Mary got back in her car and drove home to Bungle Hook, the place of so many childhood memories and family history.

Henry and Boyd Pearson attended Ada's funeral. The church bulged with people: relations and friends, some of whom were white. Henry wondered if they could be unacknowledged relatives. As he looked at the gathering, he could see various combinations of racial mixture in their coloring and facial structure: Indian, white, and Negro. He thought, slavery has created a new race of people, one that has faced rejection from so many.

Mary looked lovely in her simple black outfit. She was weeping quietly but with dignity. He was becoming conscious of his feelings for her and wished he could hold her, console her, share her grief.

Henry could feel the love and respect these people had for each other, and their pride and dignity as a group. He was proud to be associated. Henry felt a strong sense of protection toward the people of Bungle Hook. They had survived so many odds. Their noble character and strength was an inspiration at times, how they had elevated themselves. They been tested by time and circumstances.

Henry left the church quietly. He felt his loneliness return, and he was afraid he might show his feelings in some way.

*C*hapter
*E*ight

Several days after the funeral Mary returned to the Pearson mansion to talk with Henry. She fixed his lunch and he asked her to sit with him at the table so they could talk.

"Mister Henry, Grandpa's not ready to come back. He is so full of grief."

"It'll take time for him at his age, Mary. They had been together for so long. But let's talk about you. I promised Ada I would make sure you went to college as planned, no matter what. What are you going to do?"

"I really don't know. I want to go so badly, but I can't leave my Grandfather now. He is so lonely and I should take care of him. There is no one else."

"He could surely stay with one of his sons since they live so close. I don't think he would want you to give up a chance to go to college in order to stay with him."

"Grandpa would never leave his home to live

with anyone. That house and land are his pride. If he left them, he would feel less than a man. He has always admired your family, and in his way he feels the same pride of family ownership as you do. He would take such a situation as charity, and he hates charity and people who won't help themselves."

"I know, Mary. I appreciate the fact that he came here to help out for a while, and I know he stayed only because he was unable to handle the farm any longer."

"My uncles have assured him that they can handle it, but he lets them know he still owns it. His whole life is there. He'll never leave until he dies. He needs a little time to get himself straight, and I don't know whether he'll come back here or not."

"Mary, you must plan to go to school. I feel that Ada worked here specifically to earn extra money for you. She, like your grandfather, came to help when my mother was ill and my sisters and I were away at school. She remained to help my father after mother passed, and you've all become like family to us over the years. She wanted, dreamed, worked, and saved for you to have a better life than she had. Don't give it up. Try to work something out for your grandfather's care. I really feel that the best thing for him now is to work, either here or at his home. It would help him forget his grief."

"By the time the second semester begins, we will have it worked out. In the meantime, I'll stay here to help you until you can get someone else. Even if Grandpa does come back to work here, he is not much of a cook. Would that be agreeable to you?"

"I would appreciate your help, but what will Alexander say about it?"

"Since it's only for a few months. I don't think he would mind. And it might make him return."

"All right, Mary. We'll try it until it's time for you

to leave."

"Then I'll get to work. The house has been neglected too long. But I must leave earlier to prepare Grandpa's supper."

I can eat earlier, or I can go to Uncle Boyd's sometimes. You have enough to worry about. If necessary, I'll hire someone else to help you."

"Thanks, Mr. Pearson. You are understanding and patient. I'll get started now, if you are finished eating."

The next week Henry hired another woman to help Mary. She was one of the women who worked in his cannery and needed the extra money. He decided Mary could just oversee the planning and organizing of his home and meals. Ada had trained her well, and he had certain social responsibilities that Mary could handle quite comfortably. But he also had to prepare for the time when she would be leaving.

"Mary, this is Mattie Harris. She'll be helping you and will take over when you go to school."

"How are you, Mrs. Harris. I sure need your help."

Mattie did not respond, just remained silent.

"Mary, you will direct Mattie in what she is to do and she'll be responsible to you. I am leaving the running of the house to the two of you."

"Yes, Mister Henry." Mary and Mattie left to begin their chores.

The months went smoothly. Henry spent more of his time discussing concerns and interests with Mary, and she began borrowing books to read during her lonely nights. They enjoyed discussing them, and often had challenging disagreements. He enjoyed her company and the manner in which she managed his home. He began to dread the time when she would leave for school.

The memory of the turbulent fight against the

crab house lost some of its momentum since the threats hadn't worked. The council dissipated, leaving the problem of field hands unsolved. The winter social season began and the bellowing arrogance faded somewhat.

Christmas was approaching and with it Henry felt an urgent need to get away from home—and away from Mary. She had begun to invade his thoughts, his feelings, and his total being. He decided to visit a college roommate in Richmond who had often invited him to come stay for a while. He informed Mary and Mattie that they would have the holidays off since he was going away.

Mary was happy to have the time to be with her grandfather and give him a Christmas like her grandmother had. She felt this would help bring him out of the depressed state where he had been since her death.

She planned a Christmas dinner for the family and invited her two uncles, their wives, children, and Aunt Ruth. During the dinner Mary was able to discuss her college plans with her uncles.

They agreed that she should go and promised to take care of their father on weekends. Aunt Ruth said she would care for the house and at least fix his dinner. These plans were acceptable to Mary and would suffice until she came back in the summer. She felt a great relief knowing he would be cared for and she could fulfill her dream of going to college. This was the most precious gift she could have received.

Henry returned after the first of the year. He was happy that he had gone but glad to be home. The time he had spent with his friend in Richmond had fortified him, at least for awhile, against the turbulence within him. Mary would be leaving soon and things would be back to normal for him.

He and his foremen began checking the plans

for crop rotation in the spring. He asked about the workers leaving for the crab house, and the men were quite willing to talk since they would not be affected. They reported that workers forced out of their homes had moved in with relatives. He was informed also that the crab-house owners were building additional dwellings for their workers that would be completed by April.

This news left the council in a state of frenzy. The rage of the farmers began to surge with threats of violence. But Henry could sense their fear. It was frightening that their existence depended solely on Negro labor that was disappearing. He sensed impending disaster, the inevitable result of desperate men taking desperate measures.

Henry's white workers calmed down when he revealed his new plans for expansion of the mill. He knew they were not afraid of losing their jobs but were afraid of the degradation of doing Negro work. The poor whites would rather starve than take jobs they felt were only for blacks. The decades that had passed since the Civil War had not changed their attitude. Unfortunately, they had not kept pace with the times and were blind to even the few changes that the Negroes' will to survive had created.

The council called a special meeting at Boyd Pearson's home, and the call to Henry was filled with urgency. He had not planned to attend another such meeting, but his uncle demanded his presence. So he complied.

The men were subdued, but seething. Their faces revealed desperation and despair.

"I am glad you all could come," Boyd Pearson began. "We are in a hell of a mess. Our plans have backfired and we face a crisis for which I have no answer. I sure hope some of you do."

"Henry, you are in this mess with us; you'll lose

97

the same as we will. Why in hell are you so calm? You must know something you haven't told us," Lawson demanded suspiciously.

"I haven't kept anything from you," Henry said impatiently. "We've been through this before. You refuse to reconsider your plans. Don't you see we are all feeling the force of change? Our fate hangs limply in the balance at this point. I had a meeting with all my foremen and managers, and they tell me there is talk about violence against the Negroes."

Henry was interrupted by Senator Morris, "What the hell are they doing that for? We certainly did not sanction such action. That should only be used as a last resort."

"You mean you would support Klan tactics? You are a damn fool if you think that will help. It could start another Civil War and you'll lose all you've regained," Henry replied angrily.

"No, we can't let anything like that happen," Boyd Pearson agreed. "Even though the men are right."

"Don't kid yourself, Uncle Boyd; they are not doing it for you. They're doing it because theirs are the last of the working-class white man's jobs, and they are afraid they might have to do work that has always been classified 'nigger's work.' In their way they are feeling the same desperation that you are, and they're trying to protect their meager positions over the blacks. It gives them a sense of superiority, even though it's a very thin dividing line."

"Hell, Henry, they've got a right to feel that way," Lawson said, his voice rising as he spoke. "They may not be in our class, but they are still white, and that means something in this county and state, in case you've forgotten! It sounds like a lot of shit to me," he finished, almost spitting.

"Don't deceive yourself, Mr. Lawson, if it hap-

98

pens we landowners will be blamed," Henry said, trying to remain calm. "All that kind of man really wants is a job where he has control over Negroes. They need to assure themselves of their whiteness—and since that's all they have, it means more to them than money. If it didn't, many of them would have been gone by now. If you don't believe me, try offering them field jobs picking tomatoes or beans. They'd leave you in a minute."

"All right, Henry, enough of that," Boyd Pearson interjected. "Just what are we going to do. Or what are *you* going to do? Our families are tied together and have been for generations. What you do will affect me, and I want to know now what your plans are. I have a right to know. You inherited your power and position, but your father and I struggled and fought for it. I don't intend to give it up for some deserting niggers. I am not young like you. I can't start over again, and I don't intend to. You can be damn sure of that, Henry." Pearson poured a drink and wiped the perspiration from his eyes.

"I don't want to give up either, Uncle Boyd. I have never said that. None of you have listened to me. I think you'd better listen now. First, we must buy machinery that will cut down the number of hands needed in the corn and wheat fields. And we must rotate the crops and find new marketable ones that use less field labor.

"Secondly, since the crab house opens at three or four in the morning, the workers will be free by noon. Many of them will be willing to work for us after that, especially the young men who are trying to build their lives here. Which brings us to the third point: You'll have to consider paying them more than five dollars a week. It's hard to raise a family on those starvation wages. The young men and women will leave for the cities, even though they would rather stay here—their roots, like yours, are here—they don't have a choice.

"Finally, you should consider contracting with the Negroes who own their land to grow produce such as tomatoes, beans, and other small crops. They become responsible for the crops—the hardest part—and all you do is pay them and provide the trucks to pick up the produce.

"I think those are the basic considerations at this point. Adjustments or changes can take place as we go along. This is a beginning. Where it goes or how effective the plan is depends on us and how we deal with them." Henry stopped and looked around the room apprehensively. He saw pensive faces deep in productive thought for the first time since the problem began. With a sigh of relief he poured a drink and returned to his seat. He was glad to see this reaction and certainly did not want to disturb their thinking.

A few minutes later, two or three of the men began to talk quietly. The conversations continued for awhile, the voices growing louder—at times in disagreement, but not in anger. The evening ended in a spirit of hope, although no decisions had been made. They all wanted to think more about the issues and would meet the following week.

Henry felt satisfied that it was the beginning of a search for hopeful answers to questions of survival. He also knew that this was not the end of the problems between the black and white races. Where it would end even the gods didn't know. But this was the only time span in which he must live—future problems must find their own answers.

Mary came the next day with news of her decision to leave for school.

"Mister Henry, I will be leaving in two weeks. My family has worked out a plan to take care of Grandpa,

100

and I'll be back in the summer. If I can help you then, I will. I appreciate all you have done for us and I almost hate to leave, but it is something I have to do. You helped me realize that. You've been very kind and I'll remember you for it. You are so different from what they say of the whites around here."

"I'll miss you, Mary. If you need anything, please let me know. I have grown very fond of you in the time you've been here. It'll be lonely when you leave. I enjoyed our little talks, discussions, and debates—but most of all I enjoyed your warmth and friendship. Please come back. By the way, here's a book I would like you to take with you. It's one of my favorites, a book of poems by Lord Byron. I hope you enjoy them as much as I have."

Henry felt awkward. What he was saying seemed superficial, especially when there were so many tender, warm, and caring things he wanted to say. But centuries had built strong walls between them.

"I'll treasure this book, Mister Henry. I know how much you value it. Your friendship means a lot to me; it gives me a feeling of security to know you'll be here when I come back. I sincerely hope you can work out your business problems without anyone getting hurt—especially my people. There's been too much of that for too long. I must go now." Mary turned to leave. She wasn't brave enough to look into his eyes nor to let him see hers.

"I'll write you, Mister Henry, and Mrs. Harris will handle the house very well. She's a good, hard-working woman. Goodbye." She left quickly by the front door. She always would remember what her grandmother had told her: Don't be dragged through the years; walk through them proudly.

Henry executed his plans for the summer crops

relentlessly, trying to prevent violence and restore the dignity of the council while he worked to banish Mary from his thoughts. He faced resistance from some of the council members who felt his progressive plan would compromise their established positions.

In spite of the explosive situation, Henry continued his search for workers. For the first time he offered them contracts as he did with the farmers. He met regularly with Negro groups and arranged time shifts for those who would work both at the crab house and on the Pearson farm. He was disappointed when his uncle refused to join him in this revolutionary approach.

The Negroes who had been evicted began moving into the newly built shanties in Merryneck and preparing for the summer's work, that included a training program for picking and packing crab meat.

Henry purchased new trucks for picking up the tomato crops that were contracted out to Negro farmers. The word of his activities spread around the county, and when it reached the council members, some reacted with interest while others predicted failure.

A feeling of hope grew among the Negroes of the county. They had seen the nice homes of those who worked in the oyster house in the winters and on the farms in the summers. They were convinced that two salaries could help them attain the same standard of living. They wanted it so badly that they were willing to take on the exhaustive task of two jobs a day, and whole families hired themselves out for the dual labor schedule.

However, it soon became obvious that a rigid social line had been drawn between those Negroes who worked in the crab house and those who worked their own land. Farming families refused to let their sons and daughters work in Merryneck. The struggle for economic independence was creating the same conflicts between Negroes as it had between the whites and the Negroes.

The survival of the Negro farmer depended on the free labor of his children since he couldn't afford to hire help. In some instances feelings grew bitter, but most of them acquiesced in the presence of their family pride and dignity that had been drilled into them since birth. The loyal children of such families, rather than disobey, left for the city to seek better paying work since the family farm only supplied their basic needs. Every penny they earned was put back into the crops each year, leaving nothing on which to build a future and no hope of becoming independent.

The wonder of these families was the great love, pride, respect, and loyalty to their values expressed by the young who left for the cities but continued to send money home. Most of them returned each summer to spend their vacations with parents, relatives, and childhood friends.

The social life of these families was limited to relatives and close friends. They made very few friends outside the circle. Family members from throughout the area would gather for reunions every summer. Those who left their home area often continued to support their churches financially, pay the taxes, and hold onto the land.

Through the years and generations, this family bond continued to be strengthened. Grandchildren spent all their summers on the home farms until they were grown. Then great grandchildren took their places. They were constantly taught to look after each other, no matter where they were, and to help each other move up to financial success. They were taught the value of ownership and the virtue of saving money; both were ranked second in importance only to their faith in God.

When one family member moved to the city, he or she must provide for the ones who followed. They lived together until each could afford to buy his own home. This legacy included brothers, sisters, aunts, uncles, and close relatives. They built a solid foundation for future survival, for self-reliance and independence from the white society in the city. It has been called the Negroes' survival system, and it sustained them for generations, to the amazement of the whites. From this system of family networking the Negroes prospered wherever they settled. At the same time, they maintained the land of their parents, never deserting or neglecting it, always honoring the soil that nourished their roots.

*C*hapter
*N*ine

Riding home from college, Mary thought back on her semester's work. She had done well, but she knew she could have done better if she hadn't been worrying about her grandfather so much.

As the bus rolled through familiar countryside she began to think about home; her excitement built. Her grandparents' house would always be home no matter where she went. It provided the security, the love, the pride, the dignity, and the self-assurance that had sustained her family for generations. She knew one day she would probably leave to build her own life, but even if she never returned, she would carry the memory with her always. Her being was deeply rooted there, and such a bond is never broken by distance or new relationships.

Mary was jarred from her reverie by the bus driver calling her stop. The bus pulled up to the main store to let her out, and as she moved from the back of the bus she saw her grandfather waiting beside his highly polished Model T. They greeted each other warmly, then he gathered her neatly strapped bags and they drove off quickly.

Driving home Mary saw great stretches of barren farmland lying neglected and naked as if raped. The terrifying sight almost forced a scream from her lips. "Grandpa, what has happened; where is everybody?" she demanded, horrified.

"Chile, these is some terrible times. Jest about every soul is working at the crab house."

"But, what's going to happen to all this land? This section of the county has always depended on it to live."

"The land will survive, but can't tell what's gonna happen to the people. God put this land here for us to make a living. I jest don't know what'll happen since nobody wants to work in the fields no more. I sure never thought I'd live to see this day, but I am too old to worry anymore. Everything's jest changing too fast for me, chile."

"What about Mister Pearson? What has happened to him?" Her concern for Henry was apparent in her voice. "How is he, Grandpa?"

"He's well, I suppose. Don't see much of him anymore since I ain't been able to help him. I hear he's having some rough times like the rest of the big farmers, but I suppose he'll make out. A heavy shadow hangs over the land and the people, as if God was warning us," Alexander replied sadly.

"Grandpa, the warning you sense is only one of change. The land is forgiving and will live again. It has been brutalized, just as the people who worked it were. It is suffering silently from the pains of slavery and the cheap labor that cultivated it but was never allowed to reap its benefits nor enjoy the fruits it gave forth for hundred of years. I feel certain that the land, like the people who worked it, will produce new crops that are more beneficial, but they both will yield again."

"Yes, it'll yield again 'cause tis God's will, but what happens to this county or state in the meantime, chile?" Alexander asked, his tone of voice at odds with his claim of being too old to worry about the future of the land—the land that had been the mainstay of his long lifetime.

Arriving home Mary looked around at a place that was neglected and struggling for survival, like her grandfather and his people. The fields flourished with wheat and corn, however, for her uncles were working the land.

Mary entered the house with slow steps. It was like walking into an ancient mausoleum: dark, musty, all shades and curtains drawn. It was a house in deep mourning, like its owner, and waiting for death.

She walked through the house with determination, drawing all the drapes, raising the shades, and opening all the windows. Mary felt as if, by sheer willpower, she were forcing the house to come alive again. As she moved from room to room she thought, this house must live—it can't die—it must never die with all its memories and hopes. She made a promise and a prayer aloud, "Dear God, with your help I'll always keep this house alive, no matter what happens."

She went into her room, and after drawing the drapes and opening the windows, she sat and let herself drift into the past. It was here, in this simple, two-story frame house, that she always felt safe, secure, and happy. She would nurture those memories.

Her nostalgic mood was broken when Alexander brought in her bags. "I see you have opened the house. It's good to see the light and feel the air in here. I ain't felt like doing it. I sometimes feel dead since your grandmother passed. I just drift from day to day, almost hoping it'll be over soon." He stopped talking, moved to the rocking chair, and sat down.

"Mary, this house will be yours if you want it. You been so much a part of it. Your mother never liked it here, 'specially to live. Your uncles have their own places. Maybe after college you might settle down here, marry, have a family. There's a few decent young men left here, ones that come from good families and want to do something." He glanced at Mary, hoping for an answer or at least a promising look.

"I don't know, Grandpa," she answered slowly. "You know I love this place; it's home to me. But I can't say what I am going to do with my life at this time. However, it will remain in the family, I promise you that." Her grandfather looked relieved at her earnest tone.

Alexander began to rock quietly and Mary embraced him tenderly with her eyes. She watched the artistry of time, and its finished product. His fair skin was now tanned and rough, his once sparkling gray-blue eyes pale and tinted with red, and the veins stood out on tanned and wrinkled hands grown calloused from trying to make crops grow in hard, infertile land. The beautiful, straight black hair inherited from his half-Indian mother was now almost white, his once straight and proud back now bent by hard-lived years. He was indeed a masterpiece painted by time. A poet's delight.

"Come on, Grandpa," she said lovingly. "I'll fix you a good dinner. It looks like you haven't had one for awhile." She reached for his arm and they went to the kitchen.

"Grandpa, you go sit on the porch while I fix supper." Mary led him to his favorite chair on the porch.

"Don't fix much, chile. Can't eat much no more. My stomach jest gets filled with gas. Has to drink soda water most of the time. No need to trouble. Ain't no need no more." His voice trailed off into a whisper and he was asleep.

It took Mary several hours to prepare supper since she had to clean the dirty dishes first.

During the meal she began to inquire about a number of people, but mainly about Henry Pearson.

"Grandpa, what has happened to Mister Henry with so many workers leaving?" she asked quietly.

"He's a smart man, honey. He done got new machines and he's giving the workers from the crab house a little bit more money if they'll work for him after they leave their crab picking."

Mary interrupted him, "But how can they do that? Aren't they tired?"

"No, girl, you don't seem to understand. When they leaves the crab house it's only about eleven or twelve o'clock. Depends on how many crabs they get that day. They goes to work there 'round three or four in the morning, and when they gets to Mister Henry's, they almost got a full days work. They needs the money and this is the first time they ever had a chance to make so much. They's got the whole family working both places—the wives and children, even the old people are picking. The men and the children come to Mister Henry's while the women folk go home to take care of the house and fix the meals. He's the only one of the big farmers with sense enough to work this kind of plan. Them others is jest suffering." He spoke with pride about Henry Pearson, just as he always did about the family he had admired all his life.

"What about the tenant farmers who left their homes? Where do they live?"

"It seems that the owners of the crab house done built some shanties nearby for them to live in till they gets on their feet. Tain't much, jest better than nothin', but its shelter. They buys food from the store they done built down there. Seems to me them owners done jest about thought of everything."

"Mister Henry's a smart man, Grandpa. If the others had listened to him, they wouldn't be in this spot. He tried to help them, but they wanted slavery back. They got just what they deserved," she replied angrily.

Chile, that's what I always told you about people with quality. Mister Henry would have done more for the Negro a long time ago if it had not been for them others. They didn't wanta go along with him and they were friends of his family. They even called him a nigger lover to break his spirit, but saving his land and fortune was more important to him than friendship. The others'll come around, but they'll have to lose everything first. Them folks jest can't seem to change with the times. Mary, I need more lemonade. This talking is making me thirsty."

"I'll get more. It's wonderful to talk to you, Grandpa."

Mary poured the lemonade happily. Alexander seemed to be coming alive. She'd never heard him talk so much and he seemed to be enjoying it. He had always been a rather quiet person, living pretty much to himself. Grandmother had been his social link.

"Tell me, Grandpa. Why is it that our family and relatives have so much more than the others? They own land, have nice homes. I never quite understood."

"First place, chile, and you 'member this, there was never no slaves in our family, even your great grandparents were free-born. That's on my side and your grandmother's both. Besides that, we all were hard workers. We saved, bought our own land and worked it good. You comes from good stock. Never forget where you come from," he replied with a new strength she had not seen for a long time.

"Did being part white give you and our family a better chance than some of the others?" she asked softly, since she never knew how he really felt about his mixed blood.

Her grandfather remained silent as if collecting his thoughts. No one had ever asked such a question. His relatives and close friends never talked about it since they were all from the same racial mixture. It was something you accepted and lived with. Only a few had gone to pass as white.

"I suppose that may have had something to do with it. I bought this land from the Pearsons, as most people here in Bungle Hook did. They all knew we were related to the whites, and they maybe felt they owed us something." This was difficult for him, so he retreated to silence.

"But Grandpa, all the people around here with your last name are white. Don't they treat you different, although they don't acknowledge you?"

"I s'pose so. I really don't know for sure. Things like this are never talked about. It's kinda the code that black and white live by. It's better that way." Alexander got up to leave.

"Good night, Grandpa, I'll see you in the morning," Mary said to him in an understanding tone. She knew this was a touchy subject, but there were things she wanted to know that history books did not tell.

She remembered the early days when she went shopping with her grandparents at the main store in the nearest town. The owner had the same name as her grandfather. When they approached the store, the whites who were always sitting or standing outside would yell, "Oh, Randall! Here come your nigger cousins." It always filled her with rage, but she never knew how her grandfather felt. He and the store owner dealt with each other in a cordial, polite manner, passed the time of day, and said, "See you next week."

Mary's thoughts were restless that night. Sleep was sporadic even though she was very tired. Her mind seemed to settle on the Pearson house. What would it be like if the estate weren't there anymore? It had been her fairyland since she was a child, and it was the bright spot to many in that section of the county, a citadel of hope and security, especially to her family. It was a place to turn to for help or a job. People always felt they would be treated decently by the Pearsons and had learned to trust them.

To Mary, Henry had become a friend, and she thought of him that way. But it was a friendship that never could be discussed with anyone, and she felt it might be dangerous for her even to think about it. Sleep finally came and she embraced it longingly.

The bright morning sun pierced the dimness of her bedroom and reflected on the roses in the wallpaper. It said to Mary, it's day, rejoice and be glad. Its exhilarating warmth launched her on the many chores requiring her attention. She felt alive, vibrant, and happy as she dressed in a bright floral, sunback dress, braided her long hair and pinned it across the top of her head to keep cool.

When she entered the porch, she called to her grandfather, but he didn't answer. She rushed upstairs to his room, but he was not there. She went to the back yard and yelled for him. He answered from the barn, and she found him there shucking corn.

"Grandpa, I didn't hear you get up. Have you had breakfast? What time is it?" she asked, trying to account for her time.

"'Tis almost nine, chile. I been up since six. I was jest getting some feed for the chickens and pigs. I had all the breakfast I need; no need for you to bother. Figured you needed to rest." Alexander returned to his work.

Mary looked around the barn and suddenly asked in a demanding tone, "Where are the horses and the cows, Grandpa?"

"I gave them to your uncles. They was jest too much for me to care for, and I had no need of them anymore since the boys are taking care of the farm." He left the barn and Mary followed, saying no more.

Entering the house to begin her task of cleaning, she realized how a house could die if there was no life in it. To make the house really livable would be like trying to restore the dead. It was obvious her grandfather didn't live in it. He simply existed here readying for his death.

From the upstairs window she could hear Aunt Ruth giving her famous yell, "Who, ha, who, ha," to scare the crows away from her garden. Other people put up scarecrows, but she had her own style that no one ever copied. It was her own battle cry—and it worked.

Mary sighed and headed for her grandfather's room, since it needed immediate attention. She took down all the dusty curtains to wash, stripped the bed, and fluffed the feather mattress. Most of Mary's day was spent breathing life into the room where her grandparents had spent so many years together. She had always loved the dark oak, four-poster bed with its tall, carved headboard. The room was filled with products of her grandmother's gifted hands: the lace-bordered pillowcases, the long, tatted scarves that graced the dressers, the washstand and the arms and backs of the chairs.

Mary picked up her grandfather's corncob pipe. This was the favorite of his many pipes kept on a beam of the back porch. She picked up his bag of tobacco and its package of cigarette papers. Memories began to flood her mind. She remembered distinctly the first spanking he had given her, for rolling a cigarette and trying to smoke. She never smoked again. She had been fascinated by her uncles' skill and enjoyment when they rolled their cigarettes. She had always been happy that her grandfather never chewed tobacco or sniffed snuff. It was ugly and made the teeth so nasty.

After several hours of stripping rooms, Mary put all the bed linen in the dirty-clothes bag and hung the draperies and rugs on the clothesline to air out.

It was time to prepare lunch. She called Alexander to find out what he wanted. He came to the porch dripping wet with perspiration.

"Grandpa, what have you been doing?" she asked, alarmed. "You are as red as a beet and soaking wet."

"Jest working in the garden, chile. I didn't know it was so hot. That garden's about the only thing I am raising now. It needs a lot of tending." He sat down wearily, wiping his neck and face.

Mary rushed to get him some water. "Now, sit there and rest till I fix your lunch. What do you feel like eating?" she asked, moving toward the kitchen.

"Don't matter. I ain't been eating much lately. Anything you fix is jest fine. I sure could use a cool glass of water, though." He moved to the basin stand to wash his face and hands.

Mary ran to the well to draw him a fresh bucket of water. He fell into a deep, tired sleep. She was greatly concerned about his weakened condition and continued to prepare his lunch, hoping he would eat it. She went to the smokehouse and cut some ham slices, then she opened several jars of vegetables and one of peaches that had been canned by her grandmother.

Reluctantly she awakened him for lunch. He ate slowly, picking over his food and obviously forcing himself to eat. Mary watched him discreetly and saw how sick he really was. He was weak, and so drained she knew her summer would be spent here, taking care of him. After lunch, he stretched out on the porch sofa and fell back into an exhausted sleep.

The call of "Housekeepers" and a knock on the screen door told Mary that Aunt Ruth had come to call. She rushed from the kitchen to greet her.

"Come in, Aunt Ruth. I was planning to stop over, but I just haven't had the time yet." She hugged and kissed her.

"Let's go on the front porch where we can talk. Grandpa is taking a nap. I have so much to tell you." They walked through the house to the front porch.

"I see you done started the house cleaning. Menfolk don't know nothing about keeping a house. Mary, I am dying to hear about school and how you made out. I sure wished and prayed that one of mine could go, but I suppose the grandchildren'll have more of a chance."

"Aunt Ruth, it was wonderful, and I did well. I met people from all over the country, and many came from the North. There were students from my high school class in Baltimore—I think Baltimore had the highest number next to Virginia—and it was so good seeing them again. It kept me from being so scared and lonely."

"I know your grandmother would be happy. She was always so proud of you and jest loved you so much. I guess 'cause you were the first-born grandchild. Mary, I don't want to upset you none, but your grandfather ain't been doing well a'tall. I'd come to fix his dinner, but he jest wouldn't eat hardly nothing. It jest seems he is grieving himself to death. He's lost without Ada. They was together for such a long time. It's jest harder on a man to lose his wife than it is for a woman to lose her man. Taint often a woman goes before her man; most of us outlive them. I been struggling alone now going on twenty-some years."

"I think you are right about Grandpa. He's not

well. He doesn't seem to have any pain, but he's just so weak. It's awful to watch someone grieve themselves to death. It must be horrible for him. I am staying with him this summer, and I am not going to work for Mister Henry as I had planned."

"You must do what you think is best, but that money sho' would come in mighty handy for your schooling. And Mister Henry sure likes you."

"Yes, I need all the money I can get. My mother just doesn't make much, although she does well with what she gets. When I decided to go to college, I knew I had to help myself and I will. If Grandpa gets better I could work for a couple of days a week, but there is so much that needs to be done here. I can't bear to see this house go down like it is. I know how much it meant to Grandma and there is no one else to do it."

"Jest pray, chile, and things'll work out. You got youth, beauty, and brains. The Lord done blessed you with so much, I don't think He'll stop now."

"Aunt Ruth, it gets so lonely back here where we live since Grandma's gone. You are the only person I can really talk to now."

"This is a place of old people, chile. All our children are grown and gone. The few young people that was here have moved. There jest ain't none left."

"You mean they left their homes, Aunt Ruth?"

"No, chile, they didn't own nothin'. They was renting from families whose folks were dead and whose children had gone to the cities. They never belonged here; they wasn't nothing but poor trash, jest field hands going from place to place. Remember, there is jest as much difference between us and them as there is between poor whites, and you is better not mixin' with neither one."

"Aunt Ruth, you sure know a lot about everyone around here, even the whites. I am sure there are many stories you could tell about some of the rich families."

"I sure can, chile. I been here all my life, and my life itself is a real story." Ruth stopped for a reflective moment as if to bring the past and present into focus.

"I guess there is so much that has happened that nobody can talk about. There just seems to be a great wall of silence around us all," Mary introduced her favorite topic.

"Silence is safe in these parts if you wanna stay here, and that's jest about all we can do. Jest don't expect more."

"You never wanted to leave?" Mary asked in a warm, understanding tone.

"Yes, at times, but there was jest no place to go. I had eight children and we could make a livin' off the land. I had no family anywhere else that I knew about. I didn't know who my father was and my mother's family had nothin' to do with me. I even had the name of the slave woman that raised me, and she had no family either."

"Seems like things haven't changed very much between the races, even though most of us are related to the whites."

"Mary, I got to get back to work. Come see me soon. It's good to talk to you. Take good care of your granddaddy."

Mary resumed her chores in the parlor, the room that had always been like a sanctuary where the family only went on special occasions. Opening the heavy, dark draperies and raising the shades, her eyes fell on the massive organ angled across the corner of the room.

The organ had a special place in her childhood memories. When she was about six, she had gone to the revival meeting with her grandparents. She had watched fascinated as all the young people had gone to the "mourners' bench," where they sat with their

117

heads down on their arms on the back of the bench. They remained there all during the service, and near the end they would get up one at a time and declare they had gotten religion. They would go through the church shaking hands with the congregation and praising God.

Mary had wondered what the young people did while they sat there and how they knew they had been saved. On the way home she had asked her grandmother to explain. She told her that the children prayed until God spoke to them, and that's how they knew they were ready and had religion.

That evening Mary had gone into the parlor and hidden herself behind the organ. She had wanted to pray so she could get religion like the children in church. She had prayed and prayed, waiting for God to speak to her. She prayed so hard and so long without any results that she began to cry and fell into an exhausted sleep. The next morning she had gone into the kitchen and found her grandparents mourning, praying and crying. She had been terrified that something terrible had happened in the family.

They looked up and saw her and screamed. Her grandmother grabbed her and asked breathlessly where she had been. They had searched for her all night: in the fields, in everyone's houses. The whole neighborhood was up in arms about her mysterious disappearance. They embraced her, spanked her for worrying everyone, and cried over her again and again. Then she had to explain that she had been praying behind the organ for God to speak to her so she could be saved like the other children.

They forgave her, but after that, Mary knew she would never go to the mourners' bench, no matter what they did to her. It was understood that at a certain age all children had to go to the mourners' bench if they were to be saved. The dramatic disappearance of Mary was hushed up and never mentioned again. It joined the great silence that hid so many unexplainable events in their lives.

Chapter Ten

Mary rose early the next morning, fixed her grandfather's breakfast, and readied herself to see Henry.

"Mary," her grandfather asked, surprised by her appearance, "where you going dressed so fancy at this time of morning?"

"I am going to Mister Henry's to tell him I can't work for him this summer."

"I wouldn't do nothin' too hasty, chile. You don't need to spend all your time here with me. I ain't that bad off. You needs money for your schooling. You sure don't want to do nothin' to offend Mister Henry; he's been good to this family. You'd better stop and think."

"I know, Grandpa, but I must take care of you and keep this house going."

"Don't need that much help. I can manage. 'Tis true things ain't been the same with me since your grandma died, but I ain't needin' that much no more."

How weak he looked; he was aging so fast. She

could not leave him. Her grandmother would want her to take care of him. This place came first, no matter what she needed.

"Yes, Grandfather, I know how you feel, but I'll talk to him about it. Don't worry about me; I'll make out all right."

"You gonna take the car, Mary?"

"No Grandpa, I'll walk; it's such a lovely morning. I'll have a chance to think about what I am going to do. I'll be back in time to fix your lunch and I want you to rest while I am gone."

The first stretch of Mary's five-mile walk to the Pearson farm was down the small, narrow road that led out of Bungle Hook into another world. The dirt road had been developed for horses, buggies and wagons. Since it had never been enlarged, the few cars of Bungle Hook had to manage it one at a time. The three-mile road out of the dell led to the main road, but with a few short cuts through the woods and fields, the distance to the Pearson farm could be cut in half.

The long narrow road leading through Bungle Hook was like a long chapter out of history. On each side were deserted forgotten homes and lands like yesterday's passions. The barren and forsaken properties represented many hard won victories along with too much fuffering for history to record.

This little bumpy, crooked, narrow strip of earth was the road to freedom for those who traveled it. All the struggling for freedom, for survival for peace for participation in the evolution now began to fade into the unaccountable and unrelinquishing past. Here was a shadowy point in time, the eclispe of the past and present with faint-flichering reflection of tomorrow.

Mary stopped for a moment at her cousin's Sheriden's farm, at one time the center of laughter, fun and colorful peacocks. The flaunting haughty and beautiful show offs brought so much joy, the only real brightness in Bengle Hook. All the children gathered faithfully every Sunday after church, waiting hours for the great birds to spread their long brilliant feathers.

Along with the Peacock performance was a freezer of ice cream and cake. Cousin Sheriden, a giant of a man, gleamed with such pride and joy of achievement, his masterpieces, his art, his skill, his talent.

Across from cousin Sheriden was a quiet, simple white bungalow belonging to cousin Lee and his infamous wife, Esther. She provided all the gossip for the ladies at their quieting, canning, and baking sessions.

Cousin Lee had stopped farming after his children married and moved away. He spent his summers on the fishing boat, winters at the oyster house.

It was his long periods away from home when young males appeared to help with the lawns work the small garden, mainly to drive her shopping tochurch and her questionable visits to relatives.

Cousin Esther was short, chubby woman with long straight black hair that she proudly braided around her head like a crown. Her reddish brown skin glowed with rouge, her lips were brilliant red lots of cheap jewels.

During revival week all the youngsters would gather in the balcony of the church to see where she would sit since it was always a great show when she "got happy." She always sat next to a woman she didn't like. She would "get happy" and throw open both arms with great spiritual force and strike them almost unconscious.

The gossip of these yearly outbursts would last for weeks among the adults, the children had to giggle secretly or get whipped. Her behavior was always condemned as disgraceful, but that was the only discussed event of the revival.

It was here in Bungle Hook where the harsh circumstances of life lived affluently, now the dying begins without real living only it all seemed like a myth.

Her eyes filled with tears, Mary crossed the road to a small opening in the woods and a quarter mile in was the home of the Woodsons. She did not go in because the trees had grown so large as if to keep intruders out, sternly guarding it like soldiers at the entrance of a tomb.

The Woodsons had been slaves and here they had carved a home out of the wilderness given them after getting their freedom.

Recalling her visits along with the other children, she rememberd how happy they seemed, to have their visiits. They would tell exciting stories of the civil war, slavery, their marriage and their children.

Mary felt a pleasant shock of recall, their stories were told as entertainment filled with humor, only now did she wonder how they did it. Mrs. Woodson was famous for her cakes and always had one ready along with her famous peach ice cream sometimes walnuts if we would crack them.

Both the Woodsons had to be a hundred years old, they didn't know when they were born, but they were alert, active, and seemed content with their lives.

Mr. Woodson would give long lectures on his hunting ventures and had a great, but frightening display of stuffed owls along with animal heads. Their lives were like so many pages of history.

People who knew them in their new life said they didn't have any children of their own. They just raised some, about ten, those nobody wanted or strays who wondered in. They never questioned where they came from and gave them their name.

Mary began to feel the heat and walked faster,

abandoning her nostalgic moments for the reality of her purpose. Reaching the end of the narrow road, she turned and looked back. The whole area seemed to disappear, as if a magic doorway closed behind her. From the main road Bungle Hook didn't seem to exist since it could not be seen. That was probably why the people were permitted to settle there; no one could see them unless they went through the invisible doorway. It sure must have been a safe place to hide the Northern soldiers who were trying to escape or rejoin their units.

She crossed the hot tarred road for a shortcut across the Randolph's place and hoped she wouldn't stumble onto their still, as she had done once. The white moonshiners didn't like people pathing through their woods, but it was shady and saved time going to the Pearson farm.

Finally reaching the house, Mary knocked on the door of the back porch and called, "Housekeepers." Mrs. Harris came to let her in.

"Mrs. Harris, it's me, Mary. Don't you remember me?"

"Oh Lord, chile, my mind's been so busy doing so many things since you done left. Come on in, Mary. I guess you come to see Mister Henry. He's in the study working. He spends jest about all his time in there these days. I'll jest tell him you's here. Jest sit here on the porch where it's cool while I fetch him." Mattie left Mary wiping her hands and face with her long white apron.

Mary sat, thankful for the rest. She looked around—everything looked the same, no changes that she could see.

Henry rushed toward her and, without warning, grabbed her in his arms, calling her name over and over. He had lost all restraint just joy in seeing Mary.

Henry stood silently looking at her while he

124

composed himself and tried to think of an acceptable excuse for his unusual outburst. By unspoken agreement they both sat down, facing each other across the table. The silence hung in the air as they waited for Mattie to pass through.

"Mary, come into the house. I want to talk to you." They moved into the quietness of the library that also served as his study. He gently guided her to the big leather chair that she had cleaned, but never sat in.

"Let me look at you. You are even more beautiful than when you left." He pulled up a chair so that he could face her directly.

Mary was still in a state of shock. She had never seen him act or talk like this before. She was frightened and thought he must have gone mad. Henry saw the fear in her eyes and the rigidity of her body. He took her hands in his, stroking them reassuringly.

In his normal, composed manner he said, "Mary, I have missed you so much. It's been so lonely here without you. I am sorry I upset you, but I am not sorry for my actions. I don't want you to forgive me. Accept the fact that what I did was real, honest and very sincere. I don't believe you understand how much you have come to mean to me. To tell the truth, I don't quite understand it myself. But when I saw you sitting there, my feelings reached their summit and I was surprised also." He stopped stroking her hand and began gently caressing it.

Mary pulled her hands away and stood up abruptly, staring at him and not knowing what to say or do. What was happening was unreal and she must get out of there.

"Sit down, Mary. I'll get you a glass of sherry, then we'll talk."

"Mister Henry, I only came to tell you that I will not be able to work for you this summer. Grandfather is not well and needs me." She used her words like a shield and a means of escape.

"Mary, it has been hell here alone. You can't deny we are friends and there is a strong bond between us. I know about your grandfather and I respect your dedication to him, but what does that have to do with our friendship? I need you here. This place needs you. Nothing is the same when you are not here."

"Mister Henry, you are not listening to me. I said I can't work here this summer."

"I heard you, Mary. Is it possible for you to come a couple days a week, especially when my sisters come?" He was almost pleading with her and trying to dispel her fears as he talked.

"I can't work here ever again, not after today. And I don't know how I'll tell Grandpa why I can't. I really don't know myself. All I know is, something has happened and it's a force that will cause destruction."

"Mary," he interrupted, "this is not a white man taking advantage of a Negro woman. Be assured, it is not that. Yet, I am not quite sure what it is." He stopped.

They both remained silent, but their feelings had created an electrically charged atmosphere that shook their beings, their roots, and could shake the county. They both felt trapped, strained, and frightened by their emotions that couldn't be expressed. Words that couldn't be spoken were painfully repressed.

"I must leave now. I must get back in time to fix Grandpa's lunch. He'll be waiting for me." She turned to leave, grateful for a reason to escape.

"I wish you wouldn't go just yet, Mary. There are things we should talk about. I am as frightened as you are, but another time, Mary, there has to be another time."

Mary left feeling weary, strained and overwhelmed by her encounter with Henry. He had said things that many white women wanted to hear and they were things she shouldn't hear. Her thoughts were quite different on her return trip. She was engrossed with thoughts of herself, not of others. Nostalgia of the past was replaced by the reality of the present and fear of the future.

Her mother and grandmother had often talked to her about the behavior of men and what they could do to young girls, and they had especially warned her about the white men who employed them. She never thought Mister Henry could be like that; he was such a decent man, a man whom her family liked and respected. But he was still a man.

She had to admit to herself that she liked him, enjoyed talking to him, listening to him, and watching him move with assurance and strength in time of crises. There had been so much she had learned from him. Working there was an education in gracious living. "Oh, why did he have to do this! I hate him," she yelled out her anger to the trees that sheltered her.

Mary felt safe to expose her feelings, she needed the cool of the big trees. Things had happened so fast, reality, delayed, now seized her. She felt trapped, a part of some strange conspiracy against her; she felt betrayed.

"I'll never go back there," she said aloud. "Never."

Walking again, more rapidly now to make up for time lost, she thought of her grandfather waiting for her. She had reached the stage where she would add another painful memory to the community of silent, painful memories and join the rest of the people with locked-up agonies. She finally entered the opening that led back to Bungle Hook Dell. There she would be isolated and safe until she went back to school.

During lunch her grandfather broke the silence to ask, "How'd you make out with Mister Henry?"

"Fine, just fine," she said quickly, hoping to stop him there could be no further discussion of the matter. "I told him that if things worked out here, I might work a couple of days a week, especially when his sisters come."

"That's fine, chile. It's good to keep his friendship."

Mary got up and cleared the table quickly, before the conversation about Henry could resume. She noticed her grandfather was eating even less and sleeping more, which meant additional outside chores for her. He stretched out on the porch sofa and slept most of the afternoon. She welcomed the silence. She was afraid of showing her feelings until she was certain what they were.

Half asleep—half awake, the world in between birthed feeling of a transition taking place in her mind, body and soul. The half conscious feeling was like her spirit moving on without her, into unknown time dimensions with strangers in strange places, a time beyond.

Seized by terror she awakened, sat up, everything seemed strange, just lots of unfilled space. Emptiness filled her, so much empty space, and so alone and not belonging.

At the Pearson house the same human struggle was taking place in Henry. All his thoughts and feelings centered on Mary. How he longed for her. He thought of her as more than an ordinary woman. She was created to be adored, cherished, lavished, and, above all, loved. Her racial mixture had created a classic beauty that ordinary men could not appreciate. He agonized all night, struggling with feelings that were so violently opposed to his predetermined destiny. He only knew he wanted her, needed her, and had to have her whatever the cost—he knew it would be high, maybe too high.

Several weeks passed after Mary's dramatic encounter with Henry and she welcomed the quiet routine of her daily life. One morning, however, when she was upstairs cleaning the bedrooms, she thought she heard Henry's voice. Rejecting it as imagination, she continued with her work.

"Mary, Mary, come down," her grandfather yelled up the stairs. She was sure he was ill or that something had happened to him. She rushed downstairs to find him sitting on the porch talking to Henry.

"Mary, Mister Henry said his sisters were coming and he needs you to help."

"What's the matter with Miss Mattie? She's worked for him for a year now, and I have too much to do here," she exclaimed protesting.

"Don't matter about me. It'll only be a couple of weeks, chile. If Mister Henry is nice enough to give you work, you oughta take it. It's jest foolishness making such a fuss over me, and I done told him you'd come. Need no more be said. She'll be there, Mister Henry, first thing in the morning."

"Thank you, Alexander. Thank you, Mary. It'll be good having you back." He turned and left before she could respond. She had withheld more excuses for not going, but now she was enraged with him for using her grandfather's misplaced loyalty. She would tell him so at his house. He was trapping her, but it wouldn't be for long. I'll be going back to school in the fall, she thought. Mary's night was again filled with the agony of her anger toward Henry. She failed to be flattered by this last thrust his power. She would fight him. She wasn't sure how, but she would figure that out later.

Chapter Eleven

Mary arrived at the Pearson house about eight in the morning. Henry was waiting for her and Miss Mattie was fixing his breakfast.

"Come into the breakfast room, Mary, so we can discuss your duties for the next couple of weeks."

She followed him into the room and they sat down facing each other.

"You look at me as if you'd never seen me before. Am I so different that I have become a stranger to you?" He waited for an answer, sensing her anger and hostility and hoping they might help provoke some conversation.

"You are different, Mister Henry. I have never seen you like this before, and I feel you have become a stranger. That's why I can't work here. You have changed our relationship and now I don't know if it'll work. You've made it very difficult for me in my role, even a temporary one."

"Mary, your role will be as it was before. When my sisters are here you'll take charge of the house and direct Mattie in meal planning, and you'll select any other help you may need. It will work out all right. The most important thing to me is that you are here."

"You tricked me, Mister Henry. You used my grandfather to get me here and I want you to know I resent it. You have made it impossible for me to be the same. You are not the same, and you force me to change," she said angrily, but with restraint.

"Let me assure you, Mary, no harm will come to you here. We will play our roles while my sisters are here. Your anger is justified, and I deserve it, but don't worry." He caressed her hands and gazed at her endearingly.

Mary said no more about the matter, but she felt a bit more at ease. Henry's manner was hard to resist. She stood up to leave, turned a last cool glance in his direction and said, "Miss Mattie and I will begin immediately to prepare the house. I may need additional help. Who can I get since most people are working?"

"Tell me how many you will need. They will stop picking around eleven or twelve so they can come after that. Let me know when I return this evening. I'll be gone all day. As a matter of fact, I will be talking to your uncles. They have contracted to raise tomatoes for me. Goodbye, Mary." He left, taking most of the fear and anger out of her.

She and Mattie put in a full day's work in the bedrooms, but Mary made sure she would be gone before Henry returned for dinner.

That night after dinner with her grandfather, she retreated to her room to make her plans and map her strategy against her feelings for Henry. She would ask for more money, hire an unnecessary number of workers, and work shorter hours, using her grandfather as an excuse.

She wished there were some young people she could hire, especially her cousins, but most of them had headed north to work for the summer. They hired out as domestic help to wealthy families in Maine and other New England states to make money for college. The young women who were still around were taking care of their own families after they finished their day at the crab house. There were only older women left, like Aunt Ruth. She would hire her; she was strong and a hard worker for her age. Besides, she would also be a good ally, and Mary needed her strength and support right now.

Armed with her plans, she returned the next morning feeling more in control than she had the previous day. She met with Henry in the breakfast room and presented him with her plans. To her surprise, he accepted all of them without hesitation.

"Mary, I think your plans are good and I accept them. I want you to take complete charge of the house. Hire and spend what you need. I'll even give you more money than you asked for. It'll help with your college expenses."

"Thank you, Mister Henry. That's very kind of you."

"I'll be home for lunch, Mary. Let Mattie know and plan something good for this hot weather. I'll see you then." He turned and left the house.

Mary felt defeated. He had acquiesced too easily. He was taking all the fight out of her. She wondered what this man was doing. What was his game? What did he want from her? She realized she liked this new role she was playing and decided to put away her worries for now.

She and Mattie worked hard, planning for each social activity that would take place when Elizabeth and Susan were in residence. Mary found planning this year was easier and was grateful to her grand-mother for teaching her about meal planning, selecting linens, china and crystal. Ada had also taught her proper decorum; she felt confident she could play her role effectively and properly.

She felt a new excitement tingling inside. The challenge was exhilarating, but beyond that she felt that she would prove something to Mister Henry. It was as if she had silently declared war on the master of the Pearson estate.

Mary and the new workers began early to put the mansion in order for the forthcoming activities. She employed five experienced older women and made their assignments, leaving herself free to plan and supervise. The only problem for the older women was what to call her in her new role. She assured them that Mary would be fine, but they were hesitant. They saw her doing the duties of a mistress of the house. According to their previous training, she should not be referred to so familiarly. However, the fact that she was not truly the mistress caused some resentment among them, except for Aunt Ruth. Mary had assigned her to china, crystal and silver preparations, leaving the heavy work for others.

Driving home from work one evening, Ruth said, "Mary, I feel there's more going on between you and Mister Henry than one can see jest looking."

"Don't be silly, Aunt Ruth, this is just a job to me."

"I seen the way that man looks at you, chile. He's got somethin' else in mind. You better be careful," she warned.

"I'll be going back to school soon, Aunt Ruth. Don't worry," Mary assured her.

The next morning Henry met with her in the breakfast room, as usual.

"Mary, here is the list of activities planned by

my sisters. They have already made out the schedule and invitations to their guests. This summer they are planning a lawn party. I'll get some of my men to prepare the lawn, and your women will handle the food and serving. I think you have enough help to handle all the parties."

"I feel sure we can manage quite well, but will there be guests staying over?" she asked in her most efficient voice.

"Yes, there will be. My friends from Richmond. At this point, Mary, I am not sure how many. I'll let you know later."

"Will you be home for lunch, Mister Henry?" she asked, attempting to conclude the meeting.

"Yes I will, Mary. In fact I'll be staying around the house until my sisters have come and gone. I need to be here to provide assistance in matters where it will be needed. We will be working rather closely during their stay."

"Thank you, Mister Henry. I must get started now." She left him eating breakfast.

Henry's sisters arrived loaded with luggage and questions about the Pearson profit report. They had their annual meeting with himy. He explained the impact of the crab house on their business productivity, the cost of increased machinery, and the uncertainty of his new arrangements with field workers and tomato growers.

After several hours of financial discussion, they came out for lunch in a sober mood. Mattie served their lunch and quietly left.

"Henry, who is the new girl who served us and how long has she been with you? I don't remember her at all," said Elizabeth.

"Her name is Mattie. I had to have help after Ada died and Mary went away to college. She's a good, quiet, steady worker."

"She sure looks different from Mary and Ada. How long will Mary be working here? And what about her college plans?" asked Susan bluntly.

"She will return to college in late September. She came only to help me prepare for your visit. Mattie will remain permanently."

"I see you have given Mary a great deal of responsibility for one so young. She seems to have the role of mistress rather than housekeeper. Do you think that's wise, Henry?" asked Elizabeth in a voice thick with inference.

"I need Mary. She's capable and well trained by her grandmother, and she's quite intelligent. I feel lucky to have her."

Susan blurted out angrily, "Henry, if you would just get married you would have a proper mistress of your home. If this situation continues, talk will start. With all the lovely women you know, it seems strange that none of them appeals to you. You must marry, Henry, for your own protection, if nothing else. You and Mary are spending far too much time together, and she is beautiful. . ." having gone as far as she dared, her voice faded into silence.

"Susan, you are making an issue where there is none, and I don't feel it necessary to bring Mary into this conversation so much. She has her own life. I am leaving now, but I'll be back for lunch."

Mary came in during dinner to check and assist Mattie. She wore a soft green cotton dress and white, low-heeled shoes. Her makeup and hair set off her beauty. Henry thought she was an artist's dream model. She was the best of the races that had created her; he could hardly tear his eyes away.

Susan and Elizabeth exchanged glances. They could not fail to notice how Henry's eyes followed Mary longingly as she moved around the room. And her familiarity with the objects of the house gave the impression they belonged to her.

"Good evening, Miss Susan and Miss Elizabeth. I hope you have found everything satisfactory. It's nice to see you home again. Mister Henry, is everything all right? I'll be helping Miss Mattie with the dinner and then I'll be leaving, but I will see all of you in the morning." With that announcement, she left the room. Her exit was quick, precise and prevented any further conversation.

All three Pearsons were speechless. Silence covered the dinner like a veil as each attempted to cover their feelings about the evening. The meal ended abruptly, without the lingering conversation that was normal for them.

Susan and Elizabeth excused themselves hurriedly and rushed to their respective bedrooms to deal with their thoughts alone before sharing them. Henry felt a sense of relief and gratitude for their departure. He was not aware of how he looked when Mary entered the room, but he was fully aware of the blood rushing to his face and the pounding of his heart. Suddenly he felt naked, vulnerable, and afraid of the effect Mary had on him.

"Hell," he said. He jumped up from the table, rushed to his study, and poured a tall, stiff drink. He sat in his favorite chair and took a gulp, trying to recover from his emotional exhaustion. He felt drained, weak and without his usual control over the situation. It was strange to be confronted by this help-less feeling.

Susan finally went to Elizabeth's room. She found her stretched out on the pink velvet chaise lounge in a long satin lounging robe.

"I was wondering how long it would take you to get here."

"Are you thinking what I am thinking,

Elizabeth?" asked Susan, highly agitated.

"I don't know what you're thinking. Tell me what you are talking about," Elizabeth replied in a controlled voice, trying to remain calm.

"You know damn well what I am talking about. Henry and Mary of course. The way he looked at her tonight at dinner. He undressed her with his eyes and the longing in his eyes was so obvious. There were such strong vibrations between them they could have created their own volcanic eruption. Don't you dare tell me you didn't notice, because if you didn't, you're dead. I do mean dead," Susan demanded.

"I didn't think he was undressing her. I felt he was dressing her, with his passion—or love, I don't know which—to see if it fit her. I have never in my life had a man look at me like that. I was thrilled by it, but afraid, too," Elizabeth replied.

"I am afraid there is more to our dear brother than we ever knew or will know. I have wished sometimes that he wasn't my brother, and I envy the woman who gets him. But God, not Mary!" she exclaimed, horrified.

"What do you mean, Susan," Elizabeth demanded.

"You know damn well what I mean. The way he looked at her, he could never take her and leave it at that."

"I don't think she's the type that would allow it anyway, not by Henry or any man. The man who gets her will do the giving and she'll do the taking," Elizabeth said quietly and sensuously, as if enjoying the prospect. "Stop worrying, Susan. She is leaving at the end of the month and she'll be going to school for at least another three years. I am sure he'll transfer his passion to a woman of his class and race."

"But suppose he doesn't? Just think what it will do to our family name. We would be disgraced. I couldn't come back here anymore."

"Don't be silly, Susan," Elizabeth interrupted her. "The best she could be is a mistress, and white men have had them for years. I am sure our father had one. This sort of thing is accepted and expected in the South. How in the hell do you think Mary got to look like she does. You'd just better hope she's not related to us. We don't talk about such things but that doesn't mean they're not there. The one I feel sorry for is the Negro woman a white man has designs on. She doesn't have a chance; she's his and no one can or will do anything about it. The law protects him by saying he can't marry her, so he remains safe and openly continues to breed half-breeds, like Mary. So don't worry about them. Go to bed and dream about the fiery passion you'll never have." "That's what you think, my dear sister," Susan closed the door quickly, not wanting to hear a reply.

In the morning Henry left the house early, before his sisters were up or Mary had arrived. He didn't want to face any of them yet. He had to regain his composure for the big dinner party that night.

Mary arrived early, assembled her staff and gave them clear and specific instructions for the dinner party. She made sure they had brought clean white aprons and caps, not bandanas. They grumbled but assured her they had. They knew while they were changing in their quarters, Mary would be dressing in the house, in an upstairs room that Henry had set aside for her use.

"Aunt Ruth, please stay a minute." Mary took her aside as the other four left. "Aunt Ruth, I don't want you on your feet tonight, and I want you to go home for lunch and return just before the dinner at seven o'clock. You'll work with Mattie in the kitchen doing tasks that you can do sitting down. And while you're home for lunch, could you please fix something

139

for Grandpa. I won't be able to leave here today. There's just too much to do." Ruth nodded her agreement. Mary hugged her and left.

Ruth went into the kitchen to help Mattie. She found the woman in an agitated state.

"What's de matter with you, Mattie? You look like you gonna burst wide open. You are swelled up like a hog ready for slaughter."

"That Mary. She acts like she's de real mistress of dis house, puttin' on all them airs like she's better den us," she huffed and continued making dinner rolls, kneading the dough furiously.

"She's jest doin' her job, Mattie, and she'll be gone back to school soon," Ruth said reassuringly. She didn't want to get into anything with Mattie that might spoil Mary's evening.

"Knowed you'd stick up for her. All you folks in Bungle Hook think you's so much better den us 'cause you all mixed up with dem white folks. I don't see no need for Mister Henry to hire her on when I been here all the while she been gone. I sure thinks more is goin' on den you knows. But dem Pearson folks ain't lettin' no yella nigger girl take over nottin', you hear me," she bellowed at Ruth.

"No need to upset you mind, Mattie. Jest do you job and keep your big mouth shut. You been talkin' that stuff for years. It don't do no good," Ruth said as she turned away to start working. She knew the conflict between the dark and the light Negroes would go on forever. It was the reason she had never worked with them: their hate was intense. She delivered their babies; they paid her, and that was that. Most of her mid-wife work was done with the whites and Negroes she knew. The others had cruel mouths about them, so Ruth and the others who lived in Bungle Hook just avoided conflicts when possible.

140

After cocktails and hors d'oeuvres, Elizabeth and Susan's guests began to drift to the table in the dining room. They found their place cards and were seated somewhere between Henry at the head and Elizabeth at the other end.

Mary came in to supervise. She wore a white linen dress with a delicate, low-cut neckline. Her long hair was pulled into a large bun on the back of her neck, which set off the pearl necklace and matching earrings. When she walked in, all eyes turned in her direction. Although they remembered Mary from the previous year, she struck them differently somehow. Only Henry failed to look at her. Her beauty dominated dinner conversation. Mary could feel Susan and Elizabeth watching her, but she remained calm and aloof.

After dinner the men made their usual retreat into the library to talk business while the women retired to the living room to gossip. That night Mary was the main topic in both rooms. Susan and Elizabeth worked in vain to keep the conversation on other subjects. Unknowingly Mrs. Lawson helped them by announcing Martha's engagement.

While the women were cleaning up, Mary walked down to the back garden and sat in the dark to rest. The August moonlight soothed her weariness. As she was drowsing she felt someone's arms go around her. She struggled to stand, but he held her closer and kissed her. She was too tired to fight and went limp in his arms. She heard her name whispered over and over as she and Henry stood, embracing as if they were drowning and feared letting go. "Oh God, I love you, Mary," Henry whispered softly, so that only she and the night could hear. Then he left.

Trembling all over, Mary sat down until she had composed herself enough to face the others. All had gone but Aunt Ruth who would ride home with her.

"Mary, where in the name of God have you been? I was worried sick that somethin' had happened to you. Come, chile, let's jest get away from this place. I am plum wore out and I know you is too." She guided Mary out to the car and they drove home in silence. Aunt Ruth slept most of the way. Mary was grateful.

She slept that night drifting between hell and heaven. She felt what purgatory must be. Her sleep was torn between agony and ecstasy then tired sleep, to which she happily conceded.

The following morning Mary slept late and lounged in bed even though the morning sun was high. There was no need to rush to the Pearsons today. Mister Henry's sisters would be gone on their annual boating party.

At the Pearson estate, Henry rose earlier than usual. He had a special mission planned and wanted to leave before anyone awakened and missed him. He drove twenty miles to visit a justice of the peace whom he hoped could give him some answers to very perplexing questions.

He arrived at the home of Leonard Keyser, the justice of the peace who had secured his position during the reconstruction and still held it. Henry had heard many tales about this man's ancestry, but he was held in high regard politically.

A very large Negro woman answered his knock and showed him in, seated him and returned with Leonard Keyser. Henry stood as the once-tall man entered. He was now slight and bent and had only a remnant of white hair.

"Mr. Keyser, it's important that I talk to you," Henry said quickly. "My name is Henry Pearson, of the Pearsons in Forrestville."

"Yes, I know your family. Sit down and tell me your problem. Since I am the justice of the peace of

142

this district I presume you want to get married," he observed discreetly, noticing Henry's nervousness.

"Yes, I want to get married, but I want to marry a Negro." He stopped to observe Keyser's reaction.

"Young man, you do have a problem," Keyser said gravely, "one I can't do anything about. I am sure you know Virginia's laws against mixed marriages. Did you think I could change those laws?" He looked at Henry as he had looked at quite a few before who thought love would circumvent the law of legal separation of the races.

"Yes, I know the law, but I thought you could advise me on some way to comply but still make her my wife," he pleaded.

"Why would you think I would know another way other than what the law requires?" he inquired bluntly.

"My father told me you were a white man who had married a Negro." Henry waited in the shadowy silence.

"I know your family. The wealthy and powerful, Pearsons. Do you think that makes you an exception in the eyes of the law?" Leonard Keyser stared at him, looking for the strength of character that would be necessary for the battle he waged.

"No, I don't think that. But I love her beyond the flesh and I must have her. It must be legal for her protection."

"Who is she, Mr. Pearson? What woman would bring a man like you to such desperation when others just take them knowing the law will protect their actions?"

"She is the granddaughter of Alexander Randall. Do you know the family?" he asked with pride, as if talking about his own people.

"Yes, I know them well. I have known Alexander for many years. But what makes you think I could

143

help you when the law is specific and clear, Mr. Pearson?" He watched Henry's reluctance to answer, but waited.

"Mr. Keyser, I don't mean to invade your private life, but didn't you marry a Negro?" Henry was embarrassed by the question, but he had to know.

"Normally I would not answer that question, but your plight is so serious and you are so sincere that I will give you an explanation." After a long pause Keyser said, "Mr. Pearson, I married a Negro woman because I am, like many others, legally classified as Negro, although my skin is white. I was born out of wedlock to white parents. My mother's family, who were of Southern prominence, prevented the marriage. I was turned over to one of their slave women to raise as her own. You know that was not unusual around here. So you see, I had no legal problem. I married a black woman and had five children."

"But how did you get to be justice of the peace if you are Negro?"

"The woman who gave birth to me saw that I was pretty well educated and given certain privileges, but my name is that of the woman who raised me. She's my real mother."

"Have you ever seen your mother?"

"No, I have never seen either of them. I only had speculations to go on as to who they were, and I stopped a long time ago. After the Civil War I became involved in reconstruction politics and got this position without opposition. I am sure there were certain facts working on my behalf that could or would never be known. Mr. Pearson, many men such as myself were permitted a measure of short-lived political power for various reasons."

"But you kept your position when the other Negroes lost theirs."

"That is also a part of the pattern of events that

permitted me the position in the first place," Keyser replied.

"Why did you stay here?" Henry asked, puzzled.

"I have been allowed to hold this position, acquire large quantities of land, and own a very profitable business. I think I really stayed to be a reminder to the family that I existed," he answered. "I have been protected because the older families of that generation knew the circumstances of my birth and would not allow one of their own, unclaimed though I was, to go down. There was still Southern pride. You see, if I had left here, they would have wiped me out of their minds. I think it's the same way with Alexander." All the explanations were draining him and he wearily called for some drinks.

Mrs. Keyser came with a tray of glasses and a decanter of bourbon. She served them graciously.

"Mr. Pearson, I would like you to meet my wife, Mrs. Ida Keyser." He thanked her for the drinks and returned to his chair.

"Mr. Keyser, where are your children now?" Henry asked, leaning back and sipping his drink slowly. He was entranced by what he was hearing.

"My three sons work here with me. My two daughters could not take it and left for northern cities. My sons have profited very well by remaining here. My daughters come every summer and bring their children. They all will be well cared for after I am gone."

"Mr. Keyser, it's wonderful of you to tell me all this, but it must be painful."

"Not anymore, young man, not anymore." He became silent. Then, as if reading Henry's mind he said, "I know none of this has answered your question about marrying a Negro, but there are several ways you can have your young woman. One way is to leave the state. You can go north and marry her, but if you return here she can only live with you as your housekeeper, not your wife. Or you can live in separate homes, and she couldn't use your name, although your children could. It's an old custom in the South that bastard children may carry the family name, especially if they are male. It's a way of perpetuating the family name, even though their descendants would be black." He smiled.

"There's no other way?" Henry asked desperately, feeling defeated.

"I am afraid not. I'm sorry I couldn't be of more help, but remember she has a choice in this. Talk to her about what I have told you. It takes a strong and unusual woman to live that way." He showed Henry to the door.

Henry thanked him and left, confused and angry. He drove slowly back to the Pearson estate where he knew Mary would be, cleaning up from last night's party.

Chapter Twelve

"Mister Henry, I am going back home to take care of my grandfather for the rest of the summer. Miss Mattie can handle things now." She held her posture aloof.

"I understand, Mary. You know I don't want you to go, ever, but for now only. I love you, Mary, and I want to marry you, but I must find a way."

"You know I can't ever marry you, Henry." It was the first time she had ever called him by his first name, but it came easily.

"You belong here, Mary. This is the kind of life you should have, a life that beauty requires. You need to be protected and treasured. This very few men will understand or appreciate." He was startled by her laughter.

"Why are you laughing?" He felt hurt.

"I am not laughing at you, but at what you said. Our time period makes such thoughts ridiculous and insane. One learns to laugh at circumstance to survive. In my sociology class they discussed the term W.I.N. It's a term given to people like me who are white, Indian and Negro. It's meaningless since only one race is recognized: the Negro in us, even one drop. It only creates another minority for both white and black to persecute. There's no way out." Anger began to fill her eyes, her whole body became rigid. Henry watched her fill with fire, anger.

She continued, "You say you love me. That may or may not be true, but you feel free to say it to me. Would you say it to your friends and family? I can't tell my family or friends either. The barriers are so strong that such a love can't exist. I don't know whether I love you or not, the forces do not permit me to even have *thoughts* of such. Instead one concentrates only on how not to be abused by a system that considers you chattel."

"You know I don't feel or think that way about you, Mary. I love you without reason, condition or circumstance, but love is private for everyone. No one is required to make such feelings public."

"But it becomes a public issue because the law says it can't exist and the punishment is meant to destroy all who don't comply." Mary turned her head to avoid the anguish in his eyes.

He walked over to her and gently turned her around. "I know the crushing, denying feeling you described. It provokes the same anger in me, even though I am white. I am denied the right to love or marry who I want. I am a victim of the same system."

"Henry, we can't dream. The time in which we live controls what we do, and we can't overcome or fight such long-established barriers. It means destruction if we try." She began to pace around the room.

"Mary, I know fully that we live on this side of tomorrow, the wrong side, but we all hope."

"By leaping into tomorrow that means so much suffering and we can't do what we want today. Our today will not relinquish its rights to an unknown tomorrow."

"Yes, we are daring to journey into tomorrow. We are the kind of people who have the courage to move toward tomorrow without today's permission. That's how changes take place. There are different orders of man, and we are of the number who can never reconcile ourselves to such unnaturally restrictive, unjust laws."

"That sounds beautiful, Henry, but when you ignore customs, the mores of your time, you suffer isolation and rejection—so very much loneliness. Can you really call that living?"

"Mary, we can create our own world right here, and I can afford to take you anywhere in the world and buy you anything you want. Nature and man are always in conflict because nature permits all beings to survive that have the strength. It's man's laws that restrict the flow of natural instincts such as love, the one emotion that sets him apart from other animals. Must we submit to laws based on fear, ignorance, and prejudice. Don't you think there are higher laws we must obey?"

"I am not sure I have the strength or courage for such opposition. I am not sure of how I feel, so I can't make such a decision as you have. I need time to make sure this is what I want."

"We have talked enough. Take the time you need, but I'll be here waiting for you. I'll never let you go; you belong with me whatever happens."

"I must go now. I have so much to do before I leave for school." She turned to leave.

Henry stepped in front of her and put his hands on her shoulders. "Be sure that I see you before you leave. I swear I'll never do anything to degrade or tarnish the feelings we have for each other. I'll find a way for us to be together, short of starting another Civil War. Nothing will stop me, no matter what it costs personally or financially."

On the way home Mary thought how life had changed during the summer. She felt different, felt the force of Henry's love frightening her, but exciting her at the same time.

The next morning Henry drove to Richmond to visit an old classmate from Washington & Lee. Warren was a successful lawyer and Henry went to ask his advice. He went directly to Warren's office since summer month's were slow and there would be privacy.

"Come in, Henry. It's great to see you. It's been more than a year now. Sit down." He gestured to a chair.

"Thanks, Warren. I am sorry I didn't call ahead, but the urgency of my situation prompted me to act quickly."

"It sounds quite serious, Henry. I'll cancel the few appointments I have and let you have all the time you need." He left the room to give instructions to his secretary but returned quickly.

"Henry, you must be tired and you look pretty tense. Let's have a drink first. I have a feeling we are going to need it." He opened a wall cabinet and poured two tall bourbons, straight. "Here. This should relax you. We'll talk like we used to in college." They raised their glasses and took a slow swallow.

Henry did not know where to begin, so he decided to jump in feet first. "Warren, I want to marry a Negro," he blurted out.

"You what? Are you mad?" Warren shrieked and took a big gulp of his drink. "I am sorry, Henry. That was a shock. Go on."

"Warren, I know this shocks you, but I am in

love with this girl and I want her as my wife, not my mistress. I need your advice." He looked at Warren behind his massive mahogany desk and could see that he had not totally recovered his composure.

Warren got up and motioned Henry to move to a more comfortable chair where they could sit and talk.

"Henry, let's get as comfortable as possible. You are giving me the hardest case I have ever had. This is going to take awhile.

"Henry, I know you are sincere about what you say, but you are also crazy. No such thing can happen in this state, and you damn well know it."

"Yes, I know that, Warren."

"Then what in the hell can I do for you?" He was getting a little angry with his friend.

"I was hoping that you could help with some alternatives. I am determined to do this, no matter how you feel or think." He could see Warren gulping his drink.

"I believe you, Henry. That's what disturbs me. Such a thing could destroy you. I have known many men who have felt strongly about Negro women, but not enough to marry them. Society does not frown on sleeping with them but marrying them. Henry, such a thing has never been done in the South. If you marry this girl, you'll have to leave this state forever." He stopped to observe the pain on his face.

"You know I can't leave," he said in anguish.

"I know you can't, but you can have her as a mistress or a housekeeper. Why don't you settle for one of those. If you persist in following this course, you'll have to go north to marry her legally. But if you move back here, she'll still have to be your housekeeper. Even then the community would see you as a bachelor. Your family name must be carried on, and what about children? You would have no social life, and neither would she. It would mean a life of isolation for both of you. I just can't see you living like that. And remember, Henry, the women have always sought you out and will still consider you eligible. How will you keep them away?" He paused to glance at Henry; he saw no change.

"All right, Warren. I could take her north and marry her, but how do I protect her financially? I want her kept in a style that she deserves."

"What kind of woman is she, Henry? Who's her family? What makes her worth all of this?"

"I don't know, but the thought of loving her sets my soul on fire. She is life; she makes my life meaningful and rich. She comes from a good, hard-working family. Her grandparents have worked for my family off and on before my parents died. She is now attending college in Petersburg." His voice began to tremble as he talked about Mary, something he had never done with anyone before.

"Henry, if she is that kind of woman, will she go along with your plan? Have you talked to her about what you are doing?"

"No. I told her that I wanted to marry her, but she doesn't know what I am doing about it. The thought of such a relationship is frightening for her, I understand that. She has as much to lose as I do; that's one reason I want her to have some financial power, to secure her position in the community so they won't go too far."

"I can agree with that, but I am curious about what she looks like. Is she a half-breed, a mulatto or what?" The tension and anger began to fade from Warren's voice.

"She says she a W.I.N. That means white, Indian and Negro. I had never heard of that designation before. I don't think there are many people who know about that. She has the best of all three races: their strength, pride, beauty and intelligence. She's really our country in one being. Can you imagine what kind of love she commands and what joy there is in loving her?" Henry smiled boyishly.

"Henry, my friend, you are in love. This will be the love story of the century and will probably rock this nation. This story has more power than *Romeo and Juliet*. We have read of such love stories, but I never thought I'd be a part of one. I must admit, Henry, it does excite the imagination and challenges the mind." He stood up abruptly and walked over to the liquor cabinet. "All right," he said resolutely, "let's have another drink and get down to some legal facts and strategy."

He got the drinks, handed one to Henry and sat down, leaning toward his friend. "Henry, whatever you want her to have in terms of money or property must be separate from a will. Your sisters can break a will with little difficulty in this state. You will have to put them in her name now. But, what will your sisters do about this marriage? If you go through with it, there'll be the devil to pay from them. I suppose you have thought about that?" He paused for Henry's response.

"Yes, I have given it a lot of thought.I'll only give her that part of our businesses and property that is in my name only. Father did divide the estate, but I got the bulk of it since I was left with all responsibilities."

"Good, that helps. Now the money. I can open an account here in Richmond in her name. You can deposit money in it periodically. All records of property transfers must be kept here also, along with a copy of your marriage certificate. It's safe here. None of these can be filed in your county, especially in Forrestville. Can you imagine what would happen if they knew what you were doing? I hate to think of it. They would banish you, Henry."

"I am well aware and I shudder at the thought. Warren, there have been some serious changes in farming since a crab house opened and we lost most of our field hands. Many of the big farmers have not made the adjustment. So much land is going to waste. I want you to buy it up for me. Could you do that?" Confidence returned to Henry's voice as the subject fell onto familiar ground.

"You could establish a dummy company, and if you marry this girl, you could put it in her name. By the way, what is her name?"

"Mary Randall. What does that have to do with this matter?"

"The company you set up to buy the land could be the H and M company."

"Warren, you'll have to handle the purchase of the land through a well-established realtor who will not know I am involved."

"If anything happens to you, Henry, and you are married to this woman, she'll be an empress. A Southern Negro empress, that would sure put a dent in history. Some Negro men have inherited their master's or mistress' plantations, but never a woman and surely no Negro has ever done so. You are changing the history of the South, but if I weren't your friend I would strongly oppose this plan. I'd even fight you."

"I trust you, Warren. Don't let your Southern white man's pride make you betray me by discussing this with anyone, even your wife. All this must be held in the strictest confidence, and I assure you that you will be gratefully rewarded. I am sure you are aware of the seriousness of this situation and what the repercussions could be." Henry looked at Warren with a stern, questioning expression.

"Yes, Henry, I am fully aware of the seriousness of this plot and my role in it. It would ruin me if it were known that I was involved or even knew about it. We both would be run out of the state." He smiled and continued, "Now that we have that part resolved, when and how are you going to get her to go along with this crazy plan. You say she is intelligent, so I assume she is level-headed. The only way she'd agree is if she were head over heels in love with you."

"It won't be easy, but I'll convince her. I'll never give her up, no matter what I have to do."

"Somehow, Henry, I believe you will accomplish this—unfortunately. God help you both," he said and sighed. "I'll help you all I can. You're going to need a friend, and besides, I want to see how it turns out. It's like watching a movie: it can be frightening or painful, but you stay to see the end."

"Warren, I must get going. It's quite a drive back home and I've got lots of planning to do."

"Why don't you come to the house for dinner? Margaret would love to see you, and you could drive back tomorrow."

"Thanks, Warren, some other time. I don't trust myself to talk to her. It's best this way."

"I understand. You will let me know when you want the plan to go into action?"

"Yes, I'll be in touch. Thanks, it's great to have a friend like you. I appreciate your cooperation and support." They shook hands and Henry left.

His ride back to Forrestville was solemn, pensive, and lonely, but he felt good about his plans. His thoughts drifted to Mary and how she would react. He was not sure of how she felt about him; she had never said. In fact, she had evaded even the thought of such a relationship.

Mattie had dinner waiting for him and in a scolding voice said, "Der's been lots of folks here looking for you. I sure couldn't tell dem nothin' 'cause I didn't know where you was myself."

"I had to go to Richmond on urgent business so I left early. Anything important?"

"Don't suppose so. Dey said they'd talk to you

155

some other time." She left him alone to eat his dinner. Immediately after his meal, exhausted from his trip and the long, emotional session with Warren, Henry retired.

The next morning Henry arose early and drove around Forrestville looking at all the untended land. He thought the last of Negro workers could lay waste the entire South if they didn't get up off their self-indulging asses and use some sinse this all could be just a memory. He felt that all of them had lazily languished too long on the productivity of blacks, not their own, not thinking it couldn't last forever. None of the farmers had prepared for change long as slavery had been over. They felt it would be their eternal right sanctioned by God and time.

He knew one more summer of this and they would be happy to sell. Henry thought of the new crops he could grow now in demand and could be harvested by machines rather than by hand. Crops such as barley, wheat and soybeans were good possibilities. If he added some of this land to what he already had, he would own over half of the land in the county. Who would dare oppose whatever he did?

He began to plan how he would expand the cannery to include other vegetables and fruits, relying again on machinery rather than the dwindling labor force.

His thoughts wandered to the sawmill. The lumber industry was healthy and he should expand the products the sawmill produced. It seemed to him that with the older Negroes passing on and their children moving to the cities, their property could be a good source for timber in the next few years. He knew their pride of ownership would keep them from selling the land, but they might sell the timber.

The few who owned land were fiercely loyal to

their homesteads, although there were exceptions. In some cases where the family was divided over whether or not to sell, the land was sacrificed for family harmony. This happened mainly in families that owned beachfront or waterfront property, and it was usually sold too quickly and cheaply. Gradually the most valuable land in the county was being eaten up by unscrupulous land developers. The Negro families never sought advice in the matter of selling their land. Most of it went for ridiculously low prices. Henry had even bought some, just to keep it in Forrestville hands.

Henry drove to his uncle's house to see what he thought of the current situation with the land.

"Come in, Henry. It's good to see you. We didn't get a chance to talk at your dinner party. Your Aunt Bertha had a wonderful time with the girls, by the way. It's about the only time that we get a chance to see so many people. We're grateful your sisters have that get-together each year."

They sat in Boyd's study and he ordered lemonade from the housekeeper.

"Uncle Boyd, I came to ask you about how this crab house situation has affected you." He sipped his drink and watched his uncle's expression change to anger.

"How has it affected me? I'll tell you, it's just about ruined me, just like it has the rest of the big farmers around here. I think that damn crab house will fail or move to some other place before we are through. Then these nigras will come high-tailing it back to us." He started fanning and gulping angrily.

"What are your plans in the meantime, Uncle Boyd, while you're waiting for the crab house to move?" He didn't want to upset his uncle any more than he already had, so he didn't point out the obvious fact that the crab house was booming and showed no signs of closing or moving away.

"Rent out the land, I guess, or lease it or share-crop it. There are some white farmers who would just love to work this land, and maybe they can get some of that poor white trash to work since they won't have to work with Negroes." Pearson paused and looked directly at his nephew. "I really don't know what is going to happen, Henry, but I'll know by next year."

"How's your practice? That must keep you quite busy."

"Yes, it sure does. I try not to make any house calls, only in emergencies. I am getting too old to really take care of both. I'll be glad to turn the farming over to someone else. To tell you the truth, I never thought I'd live to see the day when you couldn't get Negro workers at any price. That man who runs the crab house even asked me to be their doctor to look after the workers."

"Did you accept? It sounds like a good proposition."

"Hell no! I wouldn't think of accepting the offer. I took care of those niggers almost free for years when they couldn't pay. There's not enough money to make me look after them now after what they've done!" He yelled for more lemonade.

"I would take over running your farm, but I have my hands full with my own, considering the lack of workers."

"But, Henry, you are managing better than the rest of us and this land may be yours after I am gone. My daughter sure as hell don't want it, and I am not about to let my wife's people get their hands on it. Your father and I swore that it would never leave the family, so you'd better get started having some children, Henry."

"I know, Uncle Boyd, I am thinking about it."

"You been thinking about it a damn long time.

Just don't know what you are waiting for. Everybody is talking about you living in that big house alone, especially with all the young gals just itching to get in there and be the mistress."

Henry stood up to leave. "I really must go, Uncle Boyd. I have so much to do. We can talk later about working your farm." He left quickly before his uncle could continue the discussion about his marital status.

Mary went to the bus stop to pick up her mother, who had finally agreed to come after long delays. She had written about her grandfather's condition. She wouldn't stay any longer than necessary for she really hated the country. Mary was glad she would have her mother to talk to about the situation with her grandfather. He didn't seem to be getting any better and she needed help.

The bus pulled up and Mary watched her mother walking up from the back. When she got out the sun caught her golden blonde hair and it shone like spun gold. Her blue dress highlighted sparkling blue eyes. Mary wondered why she had ridden in the back of the bus when no one would have known that she was Negro. She knew where she belonged. Color didn't change that.

Mary kissed her mother and put her suitcase in the car. They chatted constantly during the five-mile drive to Bungle Hook. The narrow, bumpy road reaffirmed her mother's reasons for not living there. She let everyone know how she felt.

"This is a dying hole," her mother said, looking at the abandoned homes. "I can't see why anyone wants to stay here. I know I'll never come back."

"Grandpa will be so glad to see you. He's been asking for you and wondering when you would be coming home."

"If you hadn't told me Papa was sick, I wouldn't be here. There's nothing else here I want or need. My dear brothers can have it." The rest of the trip was made in silence.

At the house Rachel greeted her father with a hug. He looked happy that she had finally come.

"Mother, I'll take your bag to your room while you talk with Grandpa."

At dinner the three talked of old times. The evening was filled with reminiscing about people in their lives, good and bad, alive and dead, although they avoided talking about Mary's grandmother. That memory was still too raw and painful.

"Mary, has anyone heard from Uncle Calvin or Aunt Nora?"

Her grandfather answered, "No, and don't 'spect to ever again in this life. They lives as white somewhere up north. Dey been gone since they was almost children."

"I don't blame them. I wish I had gone, too. The only thing that's stopped me is that I hate the white people too much to be one of them. Jest working for them is enough."

"Rachel, you been talking that stuff all your life. It don't help you none," her father said.

"I work for them, and I hear how they talk about us, 'cause sometimes they forget that I am colored. I come in handy when the madam wants things from stores where we can't go. They is always explaining to the children that I am one, jest to make sure they don't forget."

"Mother, why didn't you pass like Uncle Calvin and Aunt Nora?" Mary asked a question she had always wondered about.

"'Cause I didn't want to leave my family and relatives. They is about all the friends I have. It seemed like it would be a lonely life without them."

"I don't think I could do it either. I wonder if they have any children and where they are living."

"Nobody knows nothin' about them. They've only been back two times. Once for their mother's funeral, the second time for Ada's," Alexander answered.

"People ought to know what they is and be that. It can't be easy trying to be something you ain't," Rachel said.

Alexander excused himself and went up to bed. After he had gone, Mary turned to her mother and said, "Mother, Grandpa is not doing very well. He seems to perk up for awhile and then lapses back. I hope we can make some arrangements for him before I go back to school."

"Mary, you know I'll never come back here to live, and he won't come to live with me. He can't stand the city any more than I can the country. He could stay with one of my brothers, or maybe both."

"He won't leave this house. He says he is going to die here, but he just can't live here by himself."
"Well, you surely can't stay here. You're the only one of us that's got the chance to go to college, and you has to go no matter what."

"Mother, I have asked Uncle Spencer and Uncle James to dinner Sunday. Maybe we'll find an answer." Mary got up to clear the table.

Mary's uncles and their families came to dinner that Sunday. The family always enjoyed being together. They saw each other as often as they could. Alexander loved his grandchildren.

The first dinner subject was their contract with Henry Pearson. "How you boys making out with Mister Henry?" Alexander asked.

"It's not a bad deal as long as his trucks pick up the tomatoes. We sure could use more pickers," answered his younger son James.

"We will need to ask for more money if we gonna pay pickers for the kinda crop he needs. This year was a sort of trial, but if he keeps up this rate, we'll have to," stated Spencer.

"Mister Henry's a pretty fair man. Maybe if you ask him, he'll give you more," Alexander interjected weakly.

"Let's stop talking about farming and talk about Papa," Rachel interrupted. "Something gotta be done so Mary can go to school. You know I am alone now so I gotta keep working. Besides, I'd go crazy living here again."

"You know, Rachel, that Papa won't come to live with us, so what can we do?" asked James, growing tired of the same subject every time they came home.

"Seems to me that just leaves Mary to stay here with him," stated Spencer.

"Mary is gotta go to school. We have all wanted it. If she misses this chance, she'll never get another. No, it will not be her!" Rachel exclaimed angrily.

"If not Mary, then you. You've got nobody but yourself, and we've got families. We didn't go to college or even finish high school. What she gonna do but get married anyway. She sure don't need no education for that," Spencer said, banging on the table.

"Well, Mary could always go later. She's young and maybe by that time we'd be able to help her more," suggested James.

Rachel turned to Mary, "What do you think of staying here with Papa if they help you to go to school later? We sure could use some help with the fees." The offer of financial help had changed her position on the matter.

"Wish you children would jest stop this racket about me. I been taking care of myself. No need for Mary to miss her schooling. It's what her grandma dreamed about. I'm jest sick and tired of all this fuss.

162

I'm gonna die anyway. Don't make no difference if I do it alone."

Alexander got up and went upstairs to rest.

"I'll stay until he gets better. I could never leave him alone so you can all stop worrying. I am behind in classes already. It'll just take me longer to finish." Mary sensed their relief and said no more.

Spencer made his final sarcastic suggestion, "You can always work for Mister Henry when he throws them big parties since he made you a housekeeper. You sure stirred up a lotta talk. I am sure he pays you well."

The evening ended on that note, and Mary was glad to see them go. She hated her uncle for that remark. After they left, her mother questioned her about it.

"What did Spencer mean about you and Mister Henry? I don't like that kinda talk. You wouldn't be that big a fool. You got too much sense, I hope," her mother said.

"Mother, you know how people here talk. They think the white man wants all of us, or we want every white man. You know all about that, all the years of gossip about us." Mary walked away and went to bed.

Chapter Thirteen

Summer faded into fall and Mary was filled with a sense of loss. She would not be going back to school. Instead the drudgery of many hard tasks filled her days since her grandfather was unable to help. Alexander had refused many times to see a doctor. He had, as he said, surrendered to God's will.

She saw few people; only Aunt Ruth shared her loneliness and they spent hours together after dinner talking. Other times she read books that Henry would bring her, or listened to records on the Victrola.

Henry had been kind, but distant. He showed only the kindness that many of his position showed their workers, a paternal concern.

Her uncles lived only twenty-five miles away, but they came only to bring food or to take her to the store since the old Model T had stopped running. It seemed like they were miles away—it seemed like everyone was.

She began to feel defeated, trapped and deserted. Only the love of her grandparents, especially her grandmother, had kept her feelings alive. Her grandfather never got out of bed now. He complained constantly, made demands on her and talked only of the past. At times he was even cruel and abusive.

The numbness of just going on consumed her and she kept an indifferent pace with events as they developed. Thoughts of college retreated to the dark corners of her mind, along with thoughts of Henry.

Christmas was approaching. She wanted to make it a good one for her grandfather and made plans for a big family dinner. She cut a pine tree, made lovely cotton balls for snow, painted dried pine cones, cracked walnuts and ground coconut for a cake, and made wreaths of pine decorated with bright pieces of scrap material and ribbons.

The house was beautiful. Her grandmother would have loved it. On Christmas her uncles dressed her grandfather and brought him downstairs for dinner—against his loud cries of protest.

"Mary, I gotta hand it to you. You've done a great job with Papa and this house," Spencer said ingratiatingly. "I am sure glad you stayed. I don't see how we could have managed without you. I know it ain't been easy and somehow we'll make it up to you."

After dinner they all opened their gifts. Mary had none to give, but they had all brought gifts for her and Alexander. Alexander started to complain, so James and Spencer took him up to bed.

"All the fight has gone out of Papa. I sure never thought I'd live to see the day he'd quit fighting and working. Seems to me he wants to die," James said with disappointment in his voice.

"When he dies a lot of history goes with him," Spencer added. "He and Aunt Ruth are the only two left who really know what has happened in Bungle Hook. When they are gone, this place will be gone, lost to the past. All we have is what Mama and Papa have told us. It ain't written nowhere."

"The world cares little about what happened here," Mary replied quietly. "They're just our memories, and people like us don't live in tomorrow's memories, just those of the moment. But they'll be a part of my memories and I'll carry them into all of my tomorrows."

"I don't see how we can stop remembering when there are certain people around to remind you. I am talking about them white Randalls who own that big store in town. They're our cousins, and everybody knows it. Them dumb white crackers ain't gonna let anybody forget we're their 'Randall nigger cousins'," James said and poured another glass of his father's blackberry wine to wash the nasty thoughts out of his mind and the words out of his mouth.

"No need talking about what's gone before," Spencer said. "We've come this far and we'll go on. It ain't easy for us, but think what Mama and Papa lived through. It's getting late, about time for us to be getting back home. Gotta hard day tomorrow." He and his wife got up to leave. The wives had been silent through most of the conversation; they went out to round up the children. They made brief goodbyes and left.

After closing up, Mary went upstairs to her grandfather's room, pulled up a rocker and sat beside his bed watching him sleep. He wore a smile in his peaceful, childlike sleep. He looked as if he were in limbo while the gods convened to decide his time of departure. She cried quietly for the part of her that was going with him, as she had with her grandmother. She sat as if guarding him, protecting his peaceful flight into eternity.

She kept her faithful watch all night, not knowing quite why. When the morning sun burned into her

166

eyes, she looked at her grandfather. He lay in the same position he had the night before, with the same peaceful look on his face. She leaned over and touched his cooling body, his heart now stilled. He had been relieved of his burden of time and life. She laid her head on his chest and sobbed quietly, as if she feared disturbing his rest. She knew he had grieved himself to death; his longing to be with his wife was stronger than the desire to live.

She remembered she had once asked her grandmother why she had married a man ten years older than herself. She had replied that her mother liked him because he came from a good family. He had land, a house, a horse and buggy. He was a hard worker, and that was most important of all. She told Mary that love had come later, and with it respect and joy in being together.

Henry appeared at the funeral with his Uncle Boyd, as Mary knew he would. She could feel him there, and somehow she knew he would always be there.

The family buried Alexander next to his wife in the small church cemetery where vacant plots were set aside for the rest of the family. They planned to be together even beyond tomorrow. It would secure the family unity even in death.

A week later Henry came to the house like a man on a mission. "Mary," he stated, "I told you I would wait and I have, even though it has been the hardest thing I have ever done. But you are worth it, and we are going to be together forever."

"I don't know what you mean, Henry."

"Yes you do, Mary. You know I love you and we are going to get married immediately. I have worked out the plan with my lawyer, and he is going to help us. I'll never let you get away from me. I want to take care of you, protect you and lavish beautiful things on you. You're the woman for me, all any man could want or hope for in this life. All I want to know is, do you have the courage to face what we'll have to do?" he asked, watching her tenderly.

Mary could not resist the comforting feeling she got from looking into his eyes. She felt reason, logic and fear fade from her mind.

"Oh, Henry, they will destroy us!" she cried.

He took her in his arms and said reassuringly, "They may try, but they'll have a fight like they've never seen. I have made plans that will give you enough power to slow them down."

"What about my family? They'll never accept this," she cried, overwhelmed by such a decision.

"They will in time. That same power will bring them around also. Let me explain what I have worked out with my lawyer."

They sat down and Henry revealed all the daring plans he had made with Warren.

"My only problem is how to get you out of Forrestville so we can get to New York. We'll be married there and take a ship to Paris for our honeymoon. All plans have been made except leaving here, which we can't do together. You must go to Richmond alone by bus. Warren and I will meet you."

"What about my uncles?" Mary asked, not believing what she was saying or doing. She was swept up by Henry's plans and felt her resistance fading and a new source of strength emerging.

"You will sit down now and write them a note saying you are going home for awhile to see your mother. After what you've been through they'll accept that."

"What are you talking about? I thought you said I was to go to Richmond."

"Well, I just realized that it would be better if

168

you went to Baltimore and I picked you up there on the way to New York. I'll be traveling from Richmond, and since I'll have a private parlor car, no one will bother us. I'll call Warren tonight to make reservations for the train and the *Queen Mary*. We'll need a couple of days in New York for you to shop. It will be wonderful taking you to all the Fifth Avenue stores," Henry said with lively excitement. He was filled with anticipation like a child at Christmas.

Two days later Mary told Aunt Ruth that she was going home to visit her mother and wasn't sure when she would return. Aunt Ruth assured her that she understood and promised to look after everything.

Mary arrived at the Pennsylvania Station about noon. She was paged and given a telegram from Henry telling her the time his train would arrive and his car number. She had an hour to wait, so she took out the Lord Byron collection of poetry Henry had given her and tried to read. She thought poets or artists lived by their own rules, and right now it seemed like she and Henry were about to do the same. Would their lives have the same tragic ending as did so many artists and thinkers who defied the laws of their times? She drifted with her thoughts of the new adventure that lie ahead.

The train arrived on schedule and the porter helped her with her one piece of luggage. He seemed puzzled about escorting her to a private car, but he didn't say anything. Henry met her at the door of the car, tipped the porter; he escorted her inside.

Mary stopped abruptly when she saw Warren standing there. Henry saw the fear on Mary's face so he quickly introduced them.

"Mary, this is my friend Warren. He will be my best man and a witness for our wedding. Warren, this is Mary."

Warren stood up, shook Mary's hand and said

169

with formal politeness, "It's a pleasure to meet you, Miss Randall. Henry has told me so much about you. I'll be going as far as New York with you. Henry insisted that I bring some documents for you to sign after the ceremony. I'll explain them to you during the ride." He tactfully moved back to his seat and pretended to be reading.

Mary took off her plain black coat, hat and gloves. She and Henry sat opposite each other, shutting out Warren's existence.

There was a knock at the door. Mary's heart stopped, but it was the dining room waiter bringing their lunch and several bottles of champagne. The Negro waiter stared at Mary a few moments, then served them busily. His experience had taught him to see nothing and hear nothing. The waiter turned to Henry and said, "Will there be anything else, sir?"

"No, thank you," Henry said. "That'll be fine." He tipped him generously, which changed the waiter's questioning attitude to one of solicitous joy. Mary watched him and noted the sudden change, the power of money. She ate her lunch more at ease, realizing what Henry was doing for her.

Warren found it difficult to keep his eyes off Mary. They were analyzing her, trying to justify his disapproval of this relationship. He admitted she was a rare combination and had the components for a classic beauty. Her clothes were modest but tasteful, her manner friendly but aloof. She was rather poised and intelligent. Granted she was a gem of a woman, but not valuable enough to have made him take such a destructive move as Henry had taken. He thought Henry a fool; but he could afford to be, and soon she would be able to afford it also. He would not be their Brutus.

In New York they went directly to the suite at the Waldorf that Warren had reserved for them. He stayed on another floor. They did not have time to change since Warren had scheduled their meeting with the justice of the peace in their suite almost immediately.

Warren arrived with him and an Irish maid, the second witness. The ceremony was short, but the room was festooned with flowers and Mary carried a nosegay of white orchids. Henry put a wedding ring on her finger that was covered with diamonds.

The centuries of hate and distrust did not exist in their world of love. They held each other tightly, to assure themselves that nothing would ever come between them if they stayed like this.

Warren insisted that they sit down and take care of the business at hand. It shattered their tender moment. He asked Mary to read each document carefully before signing and to ask any questions she wished.

She read the papers with growing delight, signing each one Mary Pearson, then turned to Henry and said, "Oh, Henry, you have been so generous." Turning to Warren next, she looked into his disapproving eyes and said graciously, "Thank you, Warren. You have been a true friend and advisor. I do hope you will remain so through the years ahead. I feel sure we will need you." She turned and moved toward the bedroom so they could talk.

"Henry, I have two copies of the marriage certificate. One you should carry with you, and I'll keep the other with my records. I think we may need it someday. Here are your tickets for the voyage and the vouchers you requested." He turned to Mary and said, "Mrs. Pearson, you may make withdrawals on your account immediately upon your return. I will be handling all your financial affairs from now on and I'll send copies of today's transactions." He stepped toward the door, brisk and businesslike, and nodded at the newly married couple standing in the middle of the suite. "Goodbye, Henry. Have a pleasant trip, and God help you."

Henry and Mary dined leisurely in their suite after consummating their marriage without compromise or restriction. Their bodies blended in total gratification for their existence, mental and physical contact with the world extinguished by their engulfing passion. As he entered her, centuries of barriers crumbled and all lovers were set free their fever made all others non-existent and total freedom was theirs beyond time leaving the world eclipsed. No one moment could capture such rapture, they would be a part of so many tomorrows.

Later in the day they strolled through the shops along renowned Fifth Avenue, shopping for a month-long honeymoon. Clothes for a winter cruise, furs, jewels, gowns, lingerie, accessories, and perfume were purchased during an exhausting but exhilarating three days. Henry lavished his bride with expensive presents and hired several additional maids to help her with her packing. The staff of the hotel salon came to the suite to fix her hair and nails and give her a facial.

On board the *Queen Mary* time faded away, taking yesterday and tomorrow with it and leaving an endless today. They never spoke of Virginia; they thought only of the present moment. They made love in mind, body and soul—there were no separate moments, no private thoughts they didn't share with each other.

While they were dancing in Paris one night, Mary said, "Henry, no one has the right to be as happy as we are."

"Yes, we have the right, because we had the courage to take it. But we will need power to keep it.

Remember, Mary, God gave each person the right to take from life what he wants, joy or sorrow, happiness or suffering. The end for all of us is death, no matter how rich or poor, black or white. We each decide what we are willing to pay for and how much, and I am willing to pay for a happiness such as ours. We all have choices, regardless of status or race as to how we handle the events or circumstance of our lives. Mary, you must decide that this happiness is worth what we may have to pay for it if you are to bear whatever the future may hold."

"I have made the choice, Henry, although I will need your strength. There can be no turning back now. The yesterdays and all of its events would reject us. Today confirms our existence and tomorrows are unrevealing," Mary said, kissing Henry on the cheek.

"Together, Mary, we'll have many tomorrows; they won't all be joyful. We may not be able to change the time in which we live, but we have the strength and power to influence it. We can give tomorrow the gift of our love." He held her close and they drifted into sensuous silence.

They spent several days touring the Lourve. Mary was fascinated by the original paintings by artists such as Monet, Gauguin, Renoir, Raphael and Michelangelo.

They dined at the Follies Bergiere, visited Versailles and the tomb of Napoleon, and saw where Marie Antoinette was beheaded. The Arch of Triumph became their personal symbol. They visited the opera, the famous French ballet, the symphony and many salons of famous designers where Henry insisted she buy whatever struck her fancy. She wore his gifts as elegantly as she wore his love.

They bought great paintings, cases of Rothschild champagne and other French wines. They crossed the channel to London and purchased classic works of poetry by Byron, Shelley and Keats. They lavished their love on each other and shared interests to strengthen the bond that would have to sustain them throughout their lives in Forrestville.

They returned to New York and decided to stay a few days enjoying the theater, sightseeing, and just relaxing from the whirlwind European visit to fortify themselves for the return home. But the dreaded day arrived when they had to go back to face storms of uncertainty.

Warren met them at the Richmond train station. He welcomed them back and wanted to know how they planned to return to Forrestville.

"We are driving back, why do you ask?" Henry looked puzzled.

"Are you driving back at night?" Warren questioned.

"Warren, what in the hell are you trying to say?" Henry demanded.

"I thought it would be best for you two not to be seen driving into Forrestville together. There's no need to invite trouble." Warren was trying hard not to say what needed to be said.

"We are driving back to Forrestville together and immediately," Henry said firmly, taking Mary's arm and walking away.

"Henry, if you go now, I'll have to go with you." He paused, then blurted out, "It would look less conspicuous with three of us in the car. Don't you understand? You're not in New York or Paris anymore."

Mary began to feel the weight of indignation and fear as she returned to the world of the American South. How unlike Paris this was. The difference between the two countries was greater than the distance that separated them.

Henry began to understand Warren's insistence and consented to the protection his presence might provide. During the trip home, Warren talked to them about their living arrangements.

"Will Mary live in your house or in her own?"

"She'll live with me, of course," Henry replied impatiently.

"But she has never lived in your house, even when she was working for you. Won't this be an obvious change that could cause serious problems?" Warren asked pointedly.

"Our law does not forbid me from having a live-in housekeeper, Warren. His mistress can't live with him, but the law feels that a housekeeper would be of such low status she would be no threat. Therefore, having Mary live in as a housekeeper is wholly within the law. You know that, Warren."

"But won't your employees and friends talk? They'll know what's going on, especially since you are not married." Warren continued to pursue protective precautions, which irritated Henry.

"Of course they'll know. You know damn well that in a place like Forrestville they talk about everybody. There's little else to do. But don't forget I have the power to stop them economically. I can stop them from breathing."

Mary sat quietly in the back seat and listened while they discussed her future as if she weren't there. The very laws they discussed were designed to make people like her nonexistent. It was no surprise to her. She didn't mind sitting in the back, listening silently, trusting Henry to protect her. In her silence she was absorbing everything that was said, but nothing could dispel her fears about the new world she was entering and her new role.

All three of them were tired and they retired soon after they reached the Pearson estate. Henry showed Mary to his mother's luxurious bedroom that would now be hers. The arrangement had worked for his parents for years. He had no doubts it would work for them as well.

The next morning Mary arose early to supervise the breakfast. When she entered the kitchen, Mattie looked surprised and puzzled.

"Good morning, Miss Mattie," she greeted. "There will be three for breakfast this morning."

"Mary, you sure is early this morning. I didn't know you was still working here."

"Yes, Miss Mattie. I'll be staying here as Mr. Pearson's full-time housekeeper and we'll be working together as usual. You may bring the breakfast in shortly. I'll wake Mr. Pearson and his guest." With an air of authority, Mary turned and left the kitchen.

Mattie had another surprise waiting for her when she walked into the dining room to serve breakfast. Mary was seated at the table with Mister Henry and his guest. She served the two men but paused when she reached Mary.

"Mattie, serve Mary," Henry commanded.

"I ain't waiting on no nigger woman. I don't care if she is half white, she ain't no better than I am. She ain't no mistress of dis house," She said in a voice filled with hostility and left the room.

Mattie," Henry's voice stopped her, "if that is the way you feel, your services are no longer required in this house."

"Dat's jest fine with me. Everybody's talkin' about what's goin' on in dis house anyway." She stormed out.

Warren was shocked by what he had seen and heard. He couldn't believe that such hatred existed between these people.

"Henry," he said, deeply concerned, "this is much worse than I thought."

Feeling humiliated and embarrassed to the

point of tears, Mary excused herself and left the room. Henry started to follow her but Warren stopped him.

"Henry, I am here because I was concerned about protecting you, and only you. I never thought about Mary. God, she has no one to support her. She'll be persecuted by both the whites and the Negroes. I have been thinking of ways to protect you, but there are no such safeguards for her. You were damn smart to secure her financially. That'll be about all she'll have if things don't work out between you two."

"I have heard for many years, mainly from my parents, about the distrust, hostility and resentment between the dark Negro and the light, but I didn't realize it was this profound."

"I must leave, Henry. My wife will be expecting me for dinner. But I am glad I was here to witness the enormity of your plight. We must keep in constant contact, although about all I can do for you is pray. I'll call you when I get home."

After Warren left, Henry rushed to Mary, who was crying away her youth and feeling the pains of agonizing isolation. He undressed her slowly and they clung to each other, as to fortify against the cruel onslaughts yet to come.

Mary cried for several days, refusing to eat and not coming out of her room. Her tortured being struggled against the anger and the hurt that could destroy her. Henry stayed with her, holding her and trying to console her with his love.

Finally, Mary emerged from her room and came downstairs. He fixed her breakfast, which she ate silently. She looked exhausted and haggard, as if she had been in a death struggle. Abruptly she announced that she was going to her grandparents' house for awhile.

"But why, Mary?" Henry asked, gripped by the fear that she would not return. "We can work this out together better than you can alone. It won't be any easier there with all the memories of the past that live in that house."

"Henry, I need to go there. Maybe the past needs settling. Your past memories are here helping you, giving you strength. I have nothing here, not even a memory."

"Please, Mary, for God's sake don't do this to us. We can't last separately; strength comes from being together. Please don't go. I can't see how it will help solve our problems. You know the people here and how they are. What more do you need to know?" he asked.

"My grandparents faced great odds and kept going on. Maybe I need to learn how to keep going on with you, or maybe I just want to make peace with them."

"Mary, people don't keep on going because they understand, they do it because they have hope. They do it because they know no other way. We must make our own way. No one is born with directions."

"Henry, don't try to change my mind. It's made up." She continued to resist.

"All right, Mary, if you must go, I won't stop you. But understand why Bungle Hook existed and what living there meant. You can find that safety here."

"What do you mean, Henry? What do you know about it?" Her retort startled him.

"I don't know specifically or even personally about Bungle Hook, but I do know that when a group of people have the same problems and the same needs, they band together and form bonds for survival. This is what your grandparents did. They were mixed, rejected, so they built their own world. This way they could survive."

"Then what do we do, Henry, since there are only the two of us?" she asked helplessly. "Live in exile?'

"We have the advantage of money, which gives us a weapon that will help win some battles if not the war; we'll make our own rules. We'll have a hard fight or we can cling to liberty of the mind."

"Henry, you are saying we are outcasts. That's a horrible thought," Mary cried.

"Yes, in a way we are. We've broken the law, no matter how unjust it is. Aristotle said that man has to exhaust all possibilities of life, then all probabilities, and then he will find the truth. Maybe that's what we are doing."

"Whose truth, Henry?" Mary asked, becoming impatient with Henry's efforts to stop her.

"Our truth, Mary."

"What is our truth, Henry?"

"Don't you know? Come closer and I'll tell you." He put his arms around her and said softly, "We exist; we love each other, and it's your self that gives me a sense of my self. We broke a powerful law; time will not release us from its punishment. Only our minds have doors of escape, not going back there. This is your home now and all of you must exist here, not just bits and pieces."

"Dear Henry, you are trying so hard tohelp me, but I think a few days there will fortify me from other hurts to come." Mary walked wearily to the door. "Don't try to stop me. This is something I must do. Please understand."

Mary no longer felt the need or desire to explain why she wanted to leave. She felt compelled to be in her world again before she could move into another.

Henry made no effort to stop her. He was too tired, too weary, too powerless to change her mind.

179

Chapter Fourteen

Mary drove to Bungle Hook, her mind lingering on the letters she had written to her family about her marriage to Henry. She knew she would not here from them. Her mother would tear it up in a rage, seeing the fulfillment of her dreams, through her, disintegrate. She wondered if her mother would ever speak to her again.

Her uncles would destroy her letter out of fear of what it would mean to their precarious position in the community and the possible retaliation from both races.

Mary began to feel completely alone, and at the thought of the rejection ahead, she shivered. They would never believe she and Henry were married. No white man ever needed to make such a commitment to have a Negro woman.

The law had been very comfortable when Negroes were easily distinguishable and were called blacks, but after the intermingling of the races, a new law had to be passed. This one was emphatic and stated that if you had one drop of black blood you were considered a Negro.

"My God, what have I done?" Mary cried aloud in the silence of her lonely ride. The desolation of winter hung like a dark, heavy curtain of mourning over the farms. The homes were quiet; no life seemed to exist. She felt the mood of darkness as if she were standing at the point where past meets future and sky meets earth, with no direction and no where to go.

Mattie's slanderous allegations about Mary's role in the Pearson home echoed through the cloistered Forrestville community, causing a flood of speculative gossip and indignation. The leaders struggled with their versions of what they had heard. As far as the white males were concerned, especially the council members, it was Henry's right to indulge himself with his colored housekeeper. The women felt he was flaunting moral laws because he was unmarried. They openly showed their indignation toward him in church or other social situations. They would have accepted the situation, though reluctantly, if he were married, since such affairs were an accepted behavior for well-to-do husbands.

Henry knew the turmoil, but there was nothing they could do. He only had a housekeeper, and no moral obligations had ever been attached to such an arrangement.

The Negro community, on the other hand, quickly and righteously condemned Mary, saying this was what they expected of a high-yella gal. Their intense hatred supported their rejection of her and fortified Mary's isolation. They never acknowledged Henry's role in the situation since many depended on him for their livelihood.

When Mary returned to the Pearson estate, she found Henry waiting for her, looking haggard and red-eyed from sleepless nights and lack of food.

"Oh, Mary," he cried. "Thank God you came back. I was so afraid you wouldn't."

"Henry, while I was alone I remembered a few lines by Dryden: 'There is no complete and lasting pain nor complete and lasting joy.' If that were not true, who could endure life?"

Their days and nights were filled with joy and sustained on a steady diet of dreams. They dared to cherish hopeless hopes.

One night as he held Mary in his arms, Henry said softly, "We will live our lives serenely and as uneventfully as possible here in Forrestville, but we will spend most of the winter months abroad or up north. I will call Warren and have him find a woman to help you. I think it best; that way she'll not be involved in the local speculation."

"But Henry, she'll become a part of it if she stays here. What makes you think she'll feel differently toward me?" Mary asked.

"I am asking for someone who needs and wants a permanent home. We'll make her a part of our family and she can even travel with us. I don't think what the others offer her will be able to compete with what we can give her. Don't worry, I'll have Warren select and screen her carefully and brief her on the situation." Henry spoke in such a reassuring and confident manner that Mary happily agreed.

"Henry," Mary said seriously, "if the day ever comes when the law permits mixed marriages, it'll be devastating for the Negro woman."

"What do you mean, Mary?" Henry said, puzzled.

"Well, as Negro women we know the white man will never marry us. But there is the feeling that Negro

182

men will marry white women, especially those who are of some means or status, so where does that leave them? No one will ever believe we are or ever could be married, even if I told them. They'll accept the house-keeper's role or that of mistress, but never a white man of position or power marrying a Negro woman."

"Mary, are you saying that you don't object to playing the role of my housekeeper? I hate it and I am sure you do, but it makes surviving here a lot easier. You must know by now I don't feel that way or think of you that way. It's the only way we can be together. I'll move heaven and earth to make it up to you," Henry said, hoping he had convinced her.

"It's a role, Henry, and I know it's a role. There's not much difference between a housekeeper and a wife except she bears his name."

Henry was quick to respond. "If we have chil-dren they'll surely have my name. They would even if we were not married."

They slept quietly that night, glad of the silence as retreat from a painful, provoking conversation. Mary was especially grateful for the privacy of the dark to hide her fear of bringing children into such an embattled situation.

The next morning at breakfast Mary asked, "Henry, have you heard from your sisters since you wrote them about our marriage?"

"I have only received acknowledgement of their monthly shareholder's checks, nothing more," Henry replied.

"I have not heard from my mother or uncles either. It'll take time for all of them to grasp the reality of what we've done and accept it," Mary said, though she didn't believe they ever would.

"Mary, I was so glad when you came back that I have hesitated asking you what happened in Bungle

Hook."

"I can't explain, Henry. All I can say is I had to remember so many things so I could be free to forget."

"We'll say no more about it. You came back, and that's all that matters to me. You are the window of my soul; there is so much joy in your presence and so much agony in your absence. You are my light when I am awake and my dreams when I sleep. My eyes are filled with visions of you when we are apart and my life would be torment without you," Henry said, kissing her with the bright passion of a hot noon sun.

The rest of their day was spent luxuriating in passion, fulfilling love's charge willingly and totally.

A month later Harriet Moore arrived. Mary picked her up at the bus stop in front of the main store in Forrestville. It was a typical country store, housing the post office, the switchboard, and providing a front porch as a gathering place for men to see who was coming and going. They peered at Mary and Harriet in curious speculation.

Harriet was about twenty years old, short and plump with dark hair pulled back in a neat bun.

On the way home, Mary introduced herself, "Harriet, I am Mr. Pearson's housekeeper, and you will call me Mary."

"Thank you, Miss Mary. I'd like you to call me Harriet. Things should go well like dat," Harriet replied, letting Mary know she understood her position.

"I hope Mr. Warren explained our awkward situation and the importance of our private lives not being discussed," Mary probed.

"I understand. Mr. Warren explained how mighty important it was for me to keep my mouth shut, and dat I can do 'cause I been taught good by the last folks I worked for," Harriet replied with an air of understanding and assurance.

Henry met them when they arrived home and quickly escorted them into the house, away from the curious eyes of the workers. He directed them to his study to ensure total privacy. Mary sat down and Henry stood beside her while Harriet was instructed to be seated.

"Harriet, I am sure Mr. Warren and my wife have explained how unusual the situation is here. Mary is my legal wife, but it can't be known. I am sure you understand. She is known as my housekeeper and you will be our cook and help her run the house. I hope you will also be her friend and never discuss this relationship with anyone. I assure you, I'll make it worth your while as long as you remain with us. A section of the house has been closed off for your quarters. It is comfortable and equipped for your convenience. I want you to live in the house near Miss Mary at all times. You will have time off when you need it and a vacation so you can return to Richmond to see your friends and family."

"I ain't got no family in Richmond. The last folks I worked for took me from my home in South Carolina 'cause my family was too poor to take care of all twelve of us. They took me to work for them for my keep and a little spending money now 'n den. But they done left Richmond and gone back to South Carolina and had no more need of me. It jest so happens that Mr. Warren was their friend and he knew I needed to find work. Dat's how I come to get this job." Harriet expressed her gratitude for having a home and a job. She seemed to grasp the seriousness of their situation and sincerely pledged her loyalty and discretion. Since they were close in age, Mary felt she and Harriet could become friends.

"Harriet, I'll open an account for you at my bank and deposit your pay each month, or you can do it with Miss Mary's help. Anything you need or want, we'll be happy to get it for you." Henry wanted her to feel safe, secure and protected in this strange situation.

"Harriet," Mary said, "I think it would be better if you told everyone that you are from South Carolina and not Richmond. I don't think it wise since it's so close. I hope you understand, and I know you will be making friends here in Forrestville, especially in church."

"Yes Miss, I needs to join a church. I didn't get much chance in Richmond 'cause I had to work every day with no real time off. I'll only tell dem that we works together and no more, you can be sure of dat." Harriet said.

"One more important thing, Harriet. Never call me Miss or Miss Mary when others are around."

"I think it would be safer for Mary if you called her by her first name at all times, Harriet. That way you won't have to worry about forgetting," Henry suggested, to Mary's relief.

The winter loneliness was eased for Mary with Harriet's companionship. They worked together redecorating the house with the things she and Henry had bought in Paris. They shared many days talking about their families since Henry had work that kept him busy. The two women quickly became good friends. Mary felt as if Harriet were the sister she never had.

The Forrestville gossip continued, but it was more subdued since Mary and Harriet attended church together and shopped together. Henry's friends and associates stopped coming around. He only saw the men in connection with business or at the council meetings. Even his Uncle Boyd kept a respectable distance, with only business, politics or family affairs keeping them in touch.

The weary winter scene began to change and spring raised its colorful curtain to display a new cast of events and problems for the Pearsons to consider. Mary's morning sickness was the first such event and filled her with a mixture of terror and joy.

The morning of her discovery was her day of judgement. The sins of the first generation would not be passed on to the second. What forces would this stranger produce.

In the privacy of her bedroom Mary struggled with her dilemma alone for two days. How she longed for the comforting love of her grandmother. She felt lost, alone and conquered by the circumstances that her guarded love must exist. Summoning all her strength and energy, she joined Henry for a breakfast she could not eat.

"What's wrong, Mary? Don't you feel well?" Henry asked.

"I didn't sleep well. I need to get out today. I'll drive to Bungle Hook and visit Aunt Ruth. She always makes me feel better."

"All right, Mary. I'll see you later. My days will be full for the next few months. You need to visit someone like her. It'll make you feel better." Henry kissed her goodbye and left. She went into the kitchen to tell Harriet what she planned to do.

Aunt Ruth was working in her small garden, but when she saw Mary she stopped and came to greet her.

Mary hugged her tightly, like a frightened child, and said, "Aunt Ruth, I have to talk to you. You are all I have left. It's been so long since we talked."

Before she could continue, Ruth lead her into the house. "Chile, it's so good to see you. I've wondered about you and prayed many times for God to take care of you."

In the house Ruth poured two cups of coffee

187

and they sat at the table.

"Tell me, honey, what's burdening you? Your cross must be heavy. People done said some bad and mean things about you."

"What do they say in Bungle Hook, Aunt Ruth?" Mary asked, afraid of the answer.

"Things is been deathly quiet here. It's like they all in mourning 'cause they don't know you is married, not that it would make much difference. They feels a great shame, 'specially since they is all relations."

"Aunt Ruth, I have just discovered that I'm pregnant. I feel frightened for this baby. It was conceived in love, but it will be coming into a time and place that legislates hate."

"There ain't never been a time where there was not hate. I knows plenty about that. Man's laws change, dies away, but God's love is eternal. Jest 'member that, chile. Love will melt away dem hate laws, even them hate people who makes them, so you needs to have a great deal of faith. Without faith, none of us would be alive today."

Mary stood up and walked nervously around the small kitchen. Tearfully she said, "I dread the thought of my child facing so much."

"It didn't destroy me or your family neither. You may jest have to get somebody else to raise it like my mother did. These folks is so full of hate they might burn you while you sleep, burn your house and land. They jest might kill that chile. There might not be no other way to save all of you."

"I'll never do that! Never, never!" Mary shouted. "I could never give my child up. I just won't do it, even if I have to leave here."

"What do you think Mister Henry gonna say about that? He's gonna have some say in the matter."

"I haven't told him yet, and I am not going to see his uncle. I'll feel so much better if you're with me

188

when it happens."

"Girl, you know I'll be with you through this whole thing, but you're just gonna stop thinking and worrying so much and let God take care of things. He always does. Chile, if you keep going on like this you'll be sick more and you'll make that baby sick, too," Ruth said gently, stroking her hands.

"Aunt Ruth, aren't there ways to get rid of a baby before it's born? I have heard of such things. I want this baby with all my heart and soul, but I am so afraid."

"No! You can't do nothing like that. It's against God's will. I ain't never done like that in my life, even when conditions was worse than yours. God surely would punish you more than what these folks ever could do."

"You are right, Aunt Ruth. I know you are, and I don't want God against me, too. He's all I've got left. I must get back now. Thanks for bearing with me. I knew the chances I was taking when I married Henry. Our love will have to see us through this one, too. It'll have to stand many more tests."

That night at dinner, Mary told Henry with a mixture of joy and pain.

Henry shot up out of his chair, looked at Mary a few moments, then grabbed her up in his arms. "God, that's wonderful. It's what I have wanted so long. This is great news and it calls for a celebration. I hope it is a boy."

He held her tightly and kissed her ecstatically. No thoughts of the problems facing them could penetrate his joy. Henry's elation restrained Mary from revealing her tormenting fears. The night was filled with jubilant celebration.

Chapter Fifteen

Mary decided, after some deliberation, that she would spend the term of her pregnancy indoors, away from all eyes except those of Henry and Harriet. She had searched her soul for a decision that would minimize the slanderous speculations about her condition and protect the child that would be entering the world unsanctioned and without favor of family or friend.

Henry and Harriet's devotion sustained her through the life-giving period, but her sickness grew more severe, leaving her so weak that a major portion of her pregnancy was spent in bed. She did not fight this additional isolation, and the last few months of her parturition were spent in constant conversation with her unborn child.

Assuming the child would be a boy because Henry wanted one so badly, she told him about his father's strength, courage and deep capacity for love. She told him the condition of their love, their marriage, and she warned her son about the racial differences of his blood and the problems he would face. Day after day she continued her soliloquy, as if girding him for a formidable entrance into an unaccepting world.

Mary began to feel that her continuous monologue had penetrated the wall of flesh that separated them and that a lasting bond of understanding existed between them. She felt new strength, energy and peace when she added her prayers, reinforcing God's laws of love and faith.

The summer faded away, the earth spending its brilliant, vibrant colors before submerging itself in winter timelessness. Aunt Ruth had figured her delivery for December, and Mary prepared for the controversial birth.

The glory of Christmas filled the house, with Mary giving instructions to Henry and Harriet as to decorations. A decorated cradle created a ceremonial atmosphere for the Christmas child.

Aunt Ruth moved into the house with plans to stay as long as she was needed. Mary's long and painful delivery came two days before Christmas, in a house magnificently decorated as if awaiting the birth of a king.

Henry III came saucily into the world and claimed his rights by sound, not law. He was a child of longing and conflict.

Henry held his heir with pride and said, in proclamation, "This child of love will have his hereditary rights recorded legally, his property of blood, not law, will be sustained. I promise you that, Little Henry."

Henry stayed with the baby every moment for days. Ruth took charge of the child's care and slept in his room. The protective atmosphere prevailed until Spring.

The new year was celebrated with Little Henry

as the center of attention, the main attraction in the foursome's festivities. Eventually, however, the aura of celebration subsided and became tempered with imposing reality. First came the registration of the baby's birth.

Henry awakened Mary early one morning and said, "I am going to the county courthouse to register Henry's birth. Then I am going to Richmond to register him there. I am seeing Warren, Mary, to have some new papers drawn for this house. I am changing my will to make Little Henry heir to all properties I inherited from my father, including this house. That way my sisters can't sell it—since neither of them wants to live here—and it will carry the Pearson name for all future generations. If I willed it to you, they could contest it and win. You have enough property in your own name, however, and it will remain so."

Mary's days were filled with the rapture of her son. In him she could see Henry and her mother, for he was a culmination of both, a beautiful work of nature. He had to be protected and safely secured for the tomorrows of his life, his time, which she could never know. She knew she would stand at that door one day and watch him go through it alone, but for now he was hers to love, enjoy, shape, mold, and fortify.

She and Henry spent hours taking pictures of him. His hair was like golden corn silk, identical to Henry's and her mother's. He also had her mother's sparkling Danube-blue eyes, a full mouth, and high cheekbones. A classic mixture.

The birth of the baby evoked a deluge of muffled gossip, speculation, repudiation and indignity in the community. The whites took a nothing-new attitude and stored the incident with the other decadent and debasing thoughts in their minds.

Sitting in the garden sunning with Little Henry, Mary thought of him as God's child, born of God's love. He should be given to God through christening. She wanted him to have the assurance of His love and custody.

At dinner that night she said to Henry, "I want Little Henry to be christened in a church. I know it can't be mine or yours, but it must be done somehow. I read once that President Washington had fourteen or sixteen of his children by slaves christened in an Episcopal church, giving them all his name and that it's still a part of the church's records today. You know, Henry, I have never heard of a white person named Washington. It seems that only Negroes have that name. Do you think that's the reason?" She smiled.

"I am not sure, Mary, but it's a good point. However, this is not a different situation and things were looked at differently then. They were still considered his property and served him. This situation is different. The child is my son and you are my wife."

"I know, but it's almost worse because of that, especially if we want to christen him legally."

"Mary, let's plan another trip abroad this winter and we'll have him christened in a great cathedral in Paris as if he were a prince. That should make up for what can't be done here. How would you like that?" Henry asked, rather pleased with his solution.

"That'll be just wonderful. We can take Harriet to help us. I know she'll be happy to go with us and she loves the child so much. Henry, it might be a good idea to send him to school there also," she said, her mind suddenly blooming with future solutions.

"I don't know about that. I am afraid he might never come back, and this is his rightful place. He must carry on the name since he is my only heir. I'd rather select a Northern school and later a college such as Harvard, Yale or Brown, but we'll talk about that later."

"When will we leave for Paris? I'd like to be there by December to celebrate Little Henry's first birthday with his christening."

"That sounds wonderful, Mary. I'll have Warren make the necessary arrangements immediately." He was glad to see the glow of life and hope in Mary's being again.

"Henry," she said pensively, "it seems as if we are planning to conspire against our own beings."

"This love is scourged by time, Mary. It's relegated to a shadowy existence almost eclipsing us. We live by laws of untruths and those untruths become our lingering enemy."

"I know, Henry. Itlove may be born of poor judgement, but it isn't of blithe spirit. The profundity of it comes from the longings of beings created by centuries, to what end we'll never know. I firmly believe that the quality of love is born of the quality of beings and thus can't hide itself but demands of life a path to fulfillment."

"It takes more than words to confirm its worth, otherwise it would die in deceit or deception. I can only measure my love of life by having the love of my life and that's you, Mary."

He took her in his arms and their feelings touched all regions of their hearts' desires.

Little Henry was christened in the cathedral of Notre Dame in Paris on the date of his birth, and Harriet became his godmother with Warren as godfather by proxy. Henry felt satisfied that he had adequately documented his son's birth and secured his rights against future challenges.

Driving home from Richmond after their return to the states, Mary said, "Henry, what's going to happen to all this land? It's like a great disaster had struck."

"It is a disaster. The landed gentry is dying, at least in its former shape. But they can't or won't make the necessary changes. Self-indulgence and a false sense of absolute right has blinded them."

"We," Mary said, "were victims for so long we felt powerless and began to deny our own existence. That simple crab house has given the workers power they never had. Just look what has happened to these farms since they've left."

"With them gone it's us who feel powerless. The years of dependency has left devastation," Henry said as he looked around at the gloom and desolation.

"Do you think it will ever recover?"

"Yes, but it'll never be the same. It's going to take time, maybe even another generation with up-to-date ideas and skills, along with a different attitude toward workers. Time is impatient with us who can't make the necessary changes."

"Henry, what effect does this all have on you? How will you manage?"

"The way things are going, Mary, I may have to close the cannery soon. With the workers becoming more independent, I don't think they'll need additional work long. Whole families are working at the crab house, even the children. Many are building new homes, buying new cars and starting a new way of living. They are completely changing. I don't know how I can hold them."

"Henry, your friends who have the largest farms seem ashamed of the change. It keeps them frozen in time and motionless. It seems to me that they are becoming a kind of slave themselves, to their own pride, greed, ignorance, and arrogance. Change comes hard, and so many pay dearly."

195

Summer made its entrance quietly, except for the product of unguarded moments during the past winter. The weight of the unwanted child within her was a burden for Mary. It seemed as if all joy and excitement had been spent on Little Henry and there was none left for the life now taking shape in her.

She told Henry, and his feelings, too, were dull with acceptance rather than bursting with expectation. Memories of her last painful pregnancy hovered over them.

The household welcomed Mary's long-awaited delivery. Her pregnancy had been a painful ordeal. Henry sought the help of his uncle as well as Aunt Ruth.

The delivery was long, tearful and at times ominous as Mary appeared to have given up. The birth of the baby girl was like an eruption in the night, a violent momentary thrust followed by stillness. Aunt Ruth took charge of the newborn while Dr. Pearson worked on Mary. But she never recovered.

The cold dawn found Henry sitting in his empty paradise waiting for God to appear and restore Mary to the living. He held her gently in his arms, his body trembling with grief. Her death was without sense, without reason, and with no final sacrament.

Henry's state of mind frightened his uncle and he confine him to bed under heavy sedation. Aunt Ruth agreed to assume responsibility for notifying the family and making funeral arrangements.

Henry remained in his bedroom, locked in with his grief and confusion. His waking hours were filled with unanswered and unanswerable questions: Why had she died? He could not understand it. She was not a martyr, not a heroine, there was no virtue in her death. Was it guilt or innocence, would her death strengthen anything, destroy any evil? Was anything taught or learned, begun or ended?

His grief penetrated every room in the house and was borne silently by all around him. Even in death he couldn't claim Mary or openly express his love. She was returned to her world, her people, and her God.

Mary's mother came, with her two brothers and some relatives from Bungle Hook. They came out of family pride and the strong family bond that held them together, even at times like this. But Mary left them a burden of dishonor, and they bore it with mixed emotions cloaked in silence.

Henry's anger swelled, no one to console him, to share his grief for the only woman he ever loved. Now, for the first time, he understood what Mary had meant when she had to go back to her grandparents' home. He was so alone, frightened by the separation, with only memories to comfort him.

Weeks later when his anger and grief had subsided somewhat, he sent for Warren and his sister Elizabeth. It was time to make plans for his children's future.

"Warren," Henry said when his sympathetic friend arrived, "I want my daughter registered as Mary Moore. That's Harriet's last name. I am asking her to raise her. All properties that I gave Mary will now be transferred to our daughter."

"Where will they live, Henry?" Warren asked.

"They will live here, of course. She's so like Mary that I want her near me," Henry answered, moving on rapidly. "Little Henry will go away with Elizabeth. He will live in Boston until I have decided the best thing to do. Right now I can't do that."

"How will you explain his mother to him?" Warren asked.

"She died, of course. What else?" Henry answered indignantly.

"What about her? Will you tell him everything?"

"Maybe, Warren. Right now it's not important. He's a Pearson—that's what counts— and he's my son," Henry announced with pride.

Henry settled his legal matters with Warren in a cold, hard manner and dismissed him in the same way. Warren remained at the house to wait for Elizabeth and conclude the business. He was uncomfortable. Everything seemed so shadowy. it was the first time he'd ever been behind the scenes witnessing the horrible impact of such struggles. No wonder Henry is so angry, he thought. He has to give up his children and almost deny the existence of their mother to satisfy a law. The force of such cruelty made him shiver deep in sympathy for Henry's plight.

"Elizabeth," Henry said autocratically, "I am sending Little Henry to live with you until he can return here. You can bring him back when things are settled."

"Henry, you are my brother and I love you, but you can't ask me to do this. That child is part Negro. How could I explain it?" she asked.

"You don't have to explain a damn thing. He is your nephew and that's all. You've seen him. Who would question what he is? This game has been going on for so long, we all might be products of this same deception."

"Don't be ridiculous, Henry. You know we don't have any Negro blood. How could you say such a thing?" Elizabeth said indignantly.

"Warren will be guardian of their estate until they are of age. He will provide all funds necessary for Little Henry's needs, including a nurse to care for him. Elizabeth, I think you should consider doing this if you want your money to continue in the event something happens to me. There is no one else to run the business. You can't and your husband won't, and you need this income to support your high style of living.

Let's say Little Henry is your investment in the future," Henry said with surety.

Elizabeth was shocked by the change in Henry, and frightened by it. He was hard, bitter, and cold where he had been warm, loving, and gentle. She grieved for the brother she used to know. "All right, Henry," she said quietly, "I'll try it. But if it doesn't work, you will have to make other arrangements."

" When the time comes I'll tell him about his mother. We are only going to do what any family like ours would do: We are hiding family secrets like so many do. You know that's been a way of life in the South. You have not been in the North so long that you have forgotten the conspiracy of life here, Elizabeth," Henry retorted.

Then he turned to Warren and continued, "I am going to build a house for Harriet and Mary on the one section of land that belonged to Mary. I want everything in legal form, all deeds will be in her name, but it will be Harriet's when or if she leaves. I want Harriet always to have a home since she'll be acting as Mary's mother."

"No, Henry," Warren stopped him. "She will be legally Mary's mother. You are recording her birth in Harriet's name. But I'll take care of it. Just don't forget what you are doing and be absolutely sure this is what you want to do. It is forever."

"Henry," Elizabeth screamed, "you mean that woman will be your child's mother and raise her as a Negro? You can't be serious! That child has our blood."

"That's very true, Elizabeth, but I want Mary near me and that's the only way it can be done if she is to have any legal security as a human being. She's too young to be my housekeeper or a maid, and the law won't let her be my daughter and live here. If she lives here with Harriet I'll be able to see her grow up.

She will have the best. It's the best thing for a girl."

"This is hell, Henry. God, you have wrought a situation so inconceivable—and you are making us a party to it." Elizabeth began to cry.

"There's no other way, Elizabeth," Henry said sadly, softened by her tears. "If there were I would take it, but this is the way it has to be. Our laws force people to lie until many people don't really know who they are. Maybe that's not as important as living, maybe living is the only truth there is—or death."

"Oh, Henry," Elizabeth said, throwing her arms around him and sobbing. "This must be hell for you. No laws should make a man like you to do what you are doing. I never understood the cruelty of our way of life until now."

"Elizabeth, I am unable to give you a moral, tell you a prophecy, or give you the shape of tomorrow. I am uncertain and afraid. My fears are many, but they are not new. They are fears of longings, of loneliness and of unknown tomorrows. I don't want to bequeath my children the hate or intolerance that is taught and legislated by man. I want them to have love, work, joy, peace, and room to grow. I want them to have time to think without fear and long years in their tomorrows."

Henry concluded the discussion. He sought the sanctity of his grief. Warren left with Elizabeth and Little Henry, a sight forever branded on his mind. Elizabeth's description of him as had made him think of lines from a Lord Byron poem:

"Some feelings he had lately lost, or hardened;
feelings which, perhaps ideal, are so divine,
 that I must dream them real.
The love of higher things and better days.
The unbounded hope of heavenly ignorance of
 what is called the world,
and the world's ways;
The moments when we gather from a glance

More joy than from all future pride or praise."

Henry was alone at last with his anger and pain. He didn't want to see anyone or talk to anyone. Dusk fell gently and quietly that night as if to calm him, but peace was not his. Lunging from his easy chair, he screamed aloud, "Mary, I must speak to you. I must. There are things I have not said and they must be said."

He rushed to the little cemetery and threw himself over her grave, sobbing her name. "My darling," he cried, "we'll never be together again, but we'll never be apart." It was his promise, almost a pledge, filled with pain, anger and a touch of vengence.

An hour passed and the darkness engulfed his farewell. "Mary, I'll always be reaching for tomorrow, and the memory of you will be there, even in memories yet unborn."

Epilogue

"What honor is there in a woman's death!
Wronged, as she says, but helpless to revenge,
Strong in her passion, impotent of reason,
Too weak to hurt, too fair to be destroyed,
Mark her majestic fabric; she's a temple
Sacred by birth, and built by hands divine."

John Dryden